AGAINST THE EDGE

TIM HAYWOOD

Author's Note

As I begin this story, I acknowledge with gratitude that it is set
on the ancestral lands of the Coast Salish peoples, specifically
the Duwamish Tribe, who have stewarded these lands for thousands of
years. The city of Seattle, though now a bustling urban center, remains
deeply intertwined with the history, culture, and resilience of the
Duwamish people. It is important to remember that long before
skyscrapers defined the skyline, these lands were rich with ancient forests,
waterways, and a vibrant tapestry of indigenous life.

This book touches on some very difficult topics, including the loss
of loved ones, the struggles with feelings of despair
and the impact of traumatic events. I have written these elements into
the story to reflect real experiences and emotions that many people,
including children, face. If at any point you find the content distressing,
please feel free to take a break or talk to someone you trust
about your feelings.

*To Peggy Haywood—I love you, Mom.
I miss you every day.*

1

When I think about it now, it's so obvious. Nathan saved my life that day.

He'd probably disagree, but random luck wasn't the only reason I survived and so many people around me didn't. The fact is, if it weren't for him and Lucy, I might have ended up just like those people.

My mind punishes me for being a survivor. I'll wake up in the middle of the night to find that I'm curled up in a ball with my head buried below my pillow. Then, all it takes is a little spark, a tiny poke of memory from that day, and I can count on my head playing it *all* back again. If I close my eyes, the faces will pop out of the darkness, one at a time. Within seconds, I'm staring at a million of them, each with their own special look of terror. Sometimes it won't happen when I'm too tired to dream, but most nights, my brain insists on returning to that terrible day.

The field trip was going to be so much fun. Our teacher, Mr. Sharrard, had been hyping it to our class for a while, starting about a month before we went. He was constantly bugging us about permission slips and it was starting to get annoying. I'd turned mine in a long time ago.

"Listen up, fifth grade!" he'd said to our class as we ate at our desks, "a quick word, then you can return to your lunches." He thumbed through his notebook, looking through the reading glasses that lived at the end of his nose.

"There are still six of you who haven't given me your signed permission slips, and tomorrow is the final opportunity for—let's see—Lucy, Kenny, Corrie W., Lauryn, Corey S. and Zoe, to join us on our excursion. Don't make me beg, folks. It's not pretty. Some of you already know who your partners will be, but we need to have a confirmed list before we can pair up the rest of the class."

Earlier in the week, Mr. Sharrard had asked me if I was okay with being Nathan's partner for the trip, and I'd said fine. Nathan wouldn't have been my first choice, but I understood that he felt more comfortable around me than anyone else in Room 302.

Mr. Sharrard's lecture was starting to cut into lunch recess., but he didn't seem to care. He said he was determined to bring one hundred percent of the class to Olympic Sculpture Park.

"It'll be good for your souls, folks. There's art, beautiful surroundings and of course, the honor of each other's company. We will be comrades in adventure."

He'd called everybody's parents to talk about the field trip even more, including my mom on the Tuesday night before. I could hear her talking on her phone in the kitchen, using her grown-up voice and being loud enough that I knew she wanted me to hear.

"I know, right?" Mom's voice echoed in the small room. "These kids seem to have so much difficulty engaging with their surroundings. I'm starting to think that getting Theo a phone might have been a mistake. Anyway, thanks for reaching out, Mr. Sharrard—okay, Kurt—" Mom always sounded weird when she talked to my teachers.

And so, it wasn't a big surprise to learn the next day at lunch that all of Room 302 was in for the trip. "Congratulations, friends," said Mr. Sharrard. "Now no one will be on the outside looking in, as they say."

I tuned him out as he went on about field trip safety tips that I already knew. When I did, my ears locked in on a familiar but annoying noise going on behind me: the sound of Nathan eating. I turned around and felt my nose wrinkle as I looked at him. "Dude, gross," I said. "Close your mouth when you eat."

Nathan's mouth reminded me of a cartoon squirrel, with big wads of food stuffed into each cheek. His teeth raked the corn dog stick while yellow cakey bits oozed out his mouth cracks.

"Seriously, look at me for a second," I said.

He didn't.

"You should eat less gross."

"Not your business," Nathan said, carefully placing the stick on his desk and lining it up perfectly with his plastic spork. He folded his napkin and unscrunched the sleeves of his blue hoodie, one of three or four semi-identical ones he rotated through.

"Hey! Theo! Over here!" said Mr. Sharrard. "I have yet to excuse you. One more word and you can spend tomorrow helping the kindergartners get knots out of their shoelaces. Zip it!"

I turned back around, feeling a little warm. "Sorry."

"And now," Mr. Sharrard went on, "now that the trip is a go for us all, I can happily reveal our lunch destination." Closing his eyes, he tilted his head and looked at the ceiling, sniffing up a deep breath. "Ah, yes, the Olde Spaghetti Factory. Mmm, I can almost smell the piping hot garlic bread from here." He opened his eyes and scanned the first row. "Oh, never mind. I think it's just Kenny's Hot Pocket. All right then, that's it for now. Recess calls, folks."

The room got noisy right away. I looked back at Nathan and noticed that his lunch tray was clean, as usual. Some kids, well, I'd say most kids, don't like school lunches very much, but not Nathan. Even the mushy vegetables would eventually disappear into his belly.

"Ever been there?" I asked him.

"Where?"

"Olympic Sculpture Park."

"No, but the park has a scale replica of the Golden Gate Bridge," he said. More corn dog crumbs stuck to his lips, making me lick my mouth as if that would get the junk off his.

"The real bridge took four years to build," he said, "and opened to traffic on May 28, 1937. Eleven workers died during its construction."

I've known Nathan since second grade, which was when he moved here from Montana and our moms became friends. If you'd just met him, you'd think he was really quiet. Not with me, though. He talks constantly—about anything, especially stuff that has to do with bridges and structures and architecture. Or sometimes he'll just ramble off a few facts about something completely random, like all the steps that make oil into gasoline.

"Eleven died?" I said. My mom told me I should at least try to act interested. "Wow, did they just fall off or what?"

I have to say, I don't think Nathan paid much attention to my comments. Nothing seemed to keep him from popping off facts about some skyscraper or freeway or whatever. Once in a while it was kind of interesting, but other times— I don't know, he could just grind you down a little.

"Ten of the eleven fatalities occurred in a single accident on February 17, 1937, when a 5-ton work platform broke apart from the bridge and fell through the safety net."

See what I mean? And here's the other thing about him and me: once or twice a week I would have to sleep over at his place. Our moms both worked at Deany's Bar & Grill, plus they've basically been best friends since meeting each other in our apartment building's laundry room. I'd stay at Nathan's apartment when my mom worked late and his mom didn't, and him and his little sister Becky would come over when their mom worked late and mine didn't. Kind of a pain in the butt, but I'd gotten used to it, just like I'd gotten used to a lot of other new things after my parents got divorced.

The class was backed up at the door with everyone trying to get out at once. "Hey, hey, slow down, people!" Mr. Sharrard barked as he took a sip of coffee. "Put on your walking feet, friends. But please, get some exercise out there. Feel free to wear yourselves out so you don't come back in and wear me out."

Like most days, I headed for the big field to play soccer. Also like most days, the fifth grade was playing the fourth grade, which might sound unfair, but it wasn't. The younger grade had Ty Cochrane on their side, a kid who could dribble through anyone. She was new at school, and didn't just play select premier, she played select premier all-stars.

As I made my way toward the game, I watched Nathan doing what he does every recess: walking along the fence by himself. By the end of recess, he would normally go about four times around the playground while running his hand along the chain link fence. His coat was unzipped, so the back flew out and flapped behind him as one fist dug into his jacket pocket. He was big for a fifth grader, big enough that you'd think he wouldn't get picked on. Even so, he did, and usually the person that did the picking was Lucy Ratliff.

"Yo, Theo," Blase Tipton said as he ran up next to me. "We need to pass the ball better to beat the fourth graders, don't you think? Seems like everyone just wants to hog the ball and try to score."

"Definitely," I said. "I'll pass it to you if you pass it to me." As I watched Nathan make his way toward the corner of the fence, someone came running out from behind the portable. This person was headed right toward him and it only took me half a second to realize it was Lucy. "Oh, no."

She made it to him in no time. When he saw her he changed directions, but she darted around and blocked him. My head hurt at the thought of dealing with this situation. I didn't want to look like a loser, always running to protect Nathan, but it also wasn't fair for her to pick on him like she did. I left the game and walked toward the fence where she had him pinned in a corner. "So stay out of my way, freak," I heard her say as I approached them. She slammed her fist against the fence just to the side of Nathan's head, making him flinch. I kept my distance; I knew she might decide to come after me if I stuck up for him.

"Leave him alone," I said, trying to make my voice sound low and tough. The sudden fear of taking on Lucy made it come out dry and squeaky. She was bigger and faster than me. I also had no doubt that Lucy could kick my butt in a real fight, and the last thing I wanted to do was get beat up by her in front of everyone. Better to run, I figured, even if people saw.

When Lucy's head turned, her green eyes burned into me, squinting through choppy bangs of black hair, which was the same color as the shirts, coats, pants and shoes she wore every day.

"Mind your own business, Cloverdale," Lucy said, "or I'll whip your butt, too."

A clammy sweat filled my armpits and my fingers closed into loose fists. This wasn't going good.

"But since you're here," said Lucy, "I've got a message for you to pass along."

I tensed as she came closer.

"Rumor has it that we're in the same group for the field trip tomorrow."

What? I thought. *Why would Mr. Sharrard put me in her group?*

"Oh, yeah?" I said.

"Oh yeah, and it's lame." She pointed at Nathan. "I'd even rather be in his group than yours."

"Then I guess he *is* in your group," I said. "He's my partner."

"You have got to be kidding me!" Lucy's hand shot out and her knuckles stabbed into my chest.

"Ow!"

She got a hold of my ear, her nails digging in. "Stop!" I yelled.

Lucy released her hand and shoved me backwards. "And guess what else, Theo-I-Have-To-Pee-O? Your stupid mom is my partner."

"My mom? No way," I said.

"It's true. Don't act like you didn't already know."

"I didn't know, Lucy." Because if I had, I would've tried to stop it.

"Yeah, well, Mr. Sharrard just let me know that she's volunteered to be my partner. She told him that ever since me and you were in daycare together, she's 'felt a connection' with me." A soggy Cheeto crumb flew out of her mouth and hit my lip as she curled her fingers into quote marks.

It wasn't Mr. Sharrard, after all, I realized. My mom had done this to me.

"It's all a big lie, anyway," Lucy said. "It's just a way to lock me down for the whole field trip. They're making me have a babysitter."

She turned her attention back to Nathan and a dark smile grew on her face. It was a look I knew, and it made a shiver creep up my neck. She was about to cause some sort of damage. Back in fourth grade, I'd seen her grinning like that just before she busted the fire extinguisher out of its glass and sprayed it all over the kindergarten pod.

"Hey, Nathan," Lucy said. Her thumb pointed at the four square game by the play shed, where Naomi Perkins was talking and laughing with Emma and Emily. "Do you think Naomi's cute?"

"I don't know," he said, staring at the ground.

"You should go over and tell her you like fat girls like her."

A swell of rage took over my body and I yelled, "Shut up, Lucy!"

Darting toward Nathan, she faked a slap to his face, making him twitch.

"You shut up, Theo," she laughed. "Go ahead and tell her, Nathan. Girls love to hear that you still love them even when they're fat."

"No," he said, covering his ears.

I felt myself take a step toward her. "What's your problem, Lucy? He didn't do anything to you."

Lucy's black fingernails disappeared into fists and she lunged at me, driving another knobby knuckle onto my arm. "So mind your own business, tomorrow, Pee-o. And tell your mommy to mind her own business, too. I don't need a partner, especially one whose kid is a punk mama's boy like you. Hey, what's that over there?"

I looked away for a quick second and felt the tip of Lucy's boot on my shin, perfectly aimed at the middle of the bone. "Ow, oh..." I reached down and felt a fat knot already starting to form.

As I straightened back up, Lucy was already in the distance, trotting off toward the soccer game. For a while the throbbing in my shin, chest and ear competed for all the attention, but soon enough, it was all choked out by how mad I was at my mom. She'd agreed to partner with Lucy without even telling me. She had to know I hated Lucy. Everyone hated her. I felt so frustrated that I just stood there like a frozen lump, raging inside while I rubbed my tender ear. I heard Nathan's dull voice from over by the fence.

"Lucy has issues."

2

I couldn't really stay mad at Mom since we had take-n-bake pizza that night. But I still brought it up.

"Why are you Lucy's partner tomorrow?" I said. "You're going to hate it."

Mom dabbed her mouth with her napkin. "Lucy just needs a little positive attention. She seems fine when someone engages her. It's sad, really."

"Sad? Why?"

"I don't think she's got a very good support system at home."

"She's a jerk," I said. "And I'm not spending a whole day with her."

"You won't have to spend the whole day with her," Mom said. "Just stick with Nathan and I'll worry about Lucy." She took a sip of her coffee and looked at her phone. "I have to get to work. Let's clean up and I'll walk you over to Nathan's. Oh, and how about if you don't conveniently forget your toothbrush this time."

"Why do I have to go there?" I said, dragging myself along behind her as we made our way toward Building 2. "I can stay at home by myself. And their place is a total mess. And I didn't have dessert."

Mom put her arm around me and picked up her pace. "Hon, we have to overlook a few things when we're somebody's guests. We both know it's not the tidiest place in the world, but they're good people." She patted my cheek. "I'll stop at the store after work. Creamsicles?"

"Yeah," I said, "or ice cream sandwiches."

"I think what you meant to say was 'or ice cream sandwiches, please'." She stopped me as we approached their front door. "Buddy, you seem a little cranky. What's going on?"

I pulled the bottle from my backpack and took a sip of old, warm, school water. "Why can't you work during the day?"

"Honey, we've talked about this. Because it's a bar and bars are busy at night. The good news is the tips are good." She rubbed my shoulder. "Honestly, we're lucky we met Susan. She helped me get this job, which pays a lot better than my old job at the daycare did, and we've become so close that her family is our family now. Someday, I'll find a day job that works. But for now—"

"Why can't Dad send us some money?" I said. "He never pays for anything."

"He certainly—wait, how do you know that?" said Mom.

"Umm—" *Oops.*

She looked me hard in the eyes. "Tell me, Theo."

"Okay. I heard you talking to Susan about it. I was in my room. You guys were in the kitchen drinking wine. You were being loud."

Mom looked away, her head slowly drooping down. "I see."

"You said you've never seen a cent from that loser," I said.

"Well, yeah. I guess I did say that. I'm so sorry you had to hear it."

"It's okay," I said. "It's not like a big surprise or anything."

I already knew my dad was a loser.

3

The morning of the field trip, it was immediately obvious that Nathan was excited. He wouldn't stop talking as he followed me onto the bus. I chose a seat near the back and let him have the window. "Today I've got blue Gatorade," he said loudly. "Theo, do you like blue Gatorade?"

"I guess," I said.

"Why are raspberries red, but raspberry Gatorade is blue?"

"'Cause it's blue raspberry," I said.

"But raspberries aren't blue," he said, louder.

"True."

The engine fired up and we were on our way. Seattle's not always a sunny place in early May, but that morning was clear and bright. It was warm enough, in fact, that Mom only made me wear a hoodie. As soon as we pulled out of the Angelou Elementary parking lot, Nathan started reading every sign in sight. "Washington State Ferries and Seattle Waterfront, Exit 164B, right one mile." I think it was good that he was next to the window because then he could just live in his world of signs and random observations and shut out all the craziness going on inside the bus. "Theo, there's Ye Olde Curiosity Shoppe right there," he said. His finger smudged the window as he poked toward the building. "Home to Sylvester, a mummified corpse with a bullet hole in his forehead."

His voice bounced off the window glass, growing higher in volume. "The Seattle Great Wheel is 175 feet tall, the largest observation wheel on the west coast. It extends nearly 40 feet beyond the end of the pier, over Elliott Bay. 550 tons of concrete were poured to create the foundation for the—"

"Wow," I interrupted. I could see my mom laughing up front with Mr. Sharrard and the other chaperones, and it looked like they were having a lot more fun than I was. When Nathan started talking about the seawall and how it was originally patched together with landfill and old wood, I tuned him out completely and pulled my new phone out of my backpack. It had been a birthday present and I'd gotten into shooting lots of random videos and editing them with apps I'd found.

I didn't exactly have the best history with phones. I had already ruined two of them—one broke apart on the sidewalk and the other fell in the toilet. It's probably not too hard to guess how that happened. Even though I reached in immediately and fished it out, it was already too late. That incident led to a new rule in our house that banned phones from the bathroom. Before going in, I had to put it on a little tray on the hallway table. Fair enough. A few months later Mom got me a waterproof phone case for my birthday.

I wiped a smudge off the screen protector and put it away as the bus pulled into a parking lot across the street from the Sculpture Park. Mr. Sharrard stood up and made his way halfway down the aisle. "Three... two... one... eyes and ears up here, fifth grade." He kept his finger pointing to the ceiling until things got quiet. "As we all know, we're here to enjoy ourselves. Kenny, I'll wait... thank you... but we must observe a few rules:

"Number one: Stay with your partner and your chaperone at all times.

This is a big place, and we don't want anyone getting lost. If for some reason you can't find your partner, please let a chaperone know immediately."

He put his palm out. "People, I know this is very exciting, but the sooner you allow me to cover this information, the sooner we can begin our day." Mr. Sharrard's eyebrows arched as his finger pressed against his lips and grayish goatee. "Thank you. Number two: if I hear or see that you are creating a problem, you will get to spend the day with me as your partner."

His face scrunched into an angry scowl.

Uh oh, why was he mad? I wondered. Everything got quiet.

His voice was barely louder than a whisper. "And number three—

"Have fun!" he shouted.

Everyone broke into a huge laugh and at that point it wasn't getting quiet again.

"We'll meet back here at 11:30," yelled Mr. Sharrard, "and walk over to the Spaghetti Factory together. Please leave the bus calmly and—"

Everyone was jumping around, talking loud and pushing their way into the aisle. It took me and Nathan a while, since we were sitting at the very back and no one was letting anyone cut the line, but we eventually made it down the steps and onto the sidewalk. I spotted Mom, standing behind the bus with the other chaperones. Behind me I could hear Nathan's lips smacking together from another huge slurp of his blue Gatorade.

Here's something else about Nathan—the guy would stick to me like glue. He refused to walk next to me; the best I could ever see him was in the corner of my eye, but I could always tell how close he was by the loudness of his random sniffs and slurps. When we'd made it over to Mom, Nathan took another long drink, stuffed the bottle into his backpack and looked at his feet. "The Old Spaghetti Factory is in a building that once manufactured soybean glue," he said. His blue Gatorade mustache circled his blue lips and tongue. "Starting in the 1920s."

What'd he do? I wondered—*Google this stuff last night?*

"Hi, Mom." I said, figuring it wasn't a hundred percent bad having her there with us. I suppose it showed she cared and all that. Even so, it's one thing for your mom to go on a field trip with your class; it's another when she's *your* chaperone.

"Hi guys," said Mom, holding a clipboard and wearing her blue and orange Angelou Elementary sweater. "How are you, Nathan?"

"I've never been to the Old Spaghetti Factory."

She touched his arm and he flinched a little. "You'll love it. Their spumoni ice cream is the best. How about the Sculpture Park? Do you like art?"

He didn't answer. I followed Nathan's eyes up the hill to the right, where the red tips of the mini-Golden-Gate Bridge poked up in the distance. They were a brilliant red color against the bright blue morning sky. Other smaller sculptures were spread out on the grassy grounds. It was very cool and kind of weird, at the same time.

Suddenly, something hard and pointy dug into my back. I looked behind me just as Lucy's elbow drove into my chest and shoved her way around, knocking me off balance.

"What's up Pee-o?" she said, flicking my ear.

"Ow! Go find your partner," I said.

Mom stepped toward Lucy and offered her a handshake. "Hi, Lucy."

Lucy looked away, her arms limp at her sides. "Hi," she mumbled. After an awkward forever, Lucy turned and fish-flopped her hand into Mom's.

So disrespectful, I thought. Mom should've known to not even try. The rest of us knew that Lucy was lucky she even got to go on this trip. She'd already been suspended twice that year—once for leaving early and another time for telling Mr. Burton to do something, something that would have really hurt if he tried actually doing it. I felt bad that my mom had to deal with Lucy all day, but that was her choice. Lucy could be Mom's headache, not mine.

I noticed how my mom's vibe quickly transformed then from laid-back to serious once her chaperone job officially started. "Okay, everyone," she said, "when you hear your name called, please say 'here.' Theo?"

"Really?" I said. "Here."

"Nathan?"

"Here."

"Lucy?"

"Yep."

"Natalie?"

"Here."

"Caryn?"

"Here."

"Okay, that's everybody."

It was a huge win to have Caryn in our group, at least in my opinion. She was my favorite girl in fifth grade—nice, really smart, pretty—Dad always said that nobody's perfect, but he never met Caryn, either.

"Is everyone with their partner?" Mom nodded toward Lucy. "Don't be shy, partner. Come on over and stand by me."

Lucy moved about two inches closer and stopped.

"Okay," Mom said, "like Mr. Sharrard said, we can go anywhere we want, but let's try to stay together, okay? I only have one set of eyes, so I'm counting on you to be sure that you can see me at all times."

I looked around. The park was huge, built along the side of a hill that sloped toward Elliott Bay and stretched all the way down to where a massive cruise ship was docked. In front of us was a sculpture of a tall, stretched-out human face, and a little further past it was the biggest pink eraser I'd ever seen. It made me wonder who thought an eraser was art when it was really just a smudgy, rubbery thing that never totally got rid of your mistakes. Behind the eraser was a silver tree. If it was green it would've looked like a real tree, but the whole thing—even every single branch—was made of metal. Lucy was already down under it, jumping and trying to grab the lowest limb. I couldn't see her face, but my guess was that it was already wearing that dark smile.

"Lucy!" Mom took off jogging toward the tree, then jerked to a stop and faced our group. "Everyone stay here, please. I'll be right back." She wasn't fast enough to catch Lucy, and by the time Mom got to the tree, Lucy was up inside the it, bouncing around on its thin limbs.

"Lucy, you need to get down." Mom's voice was calm-ish. "Those branches are too thin for your weight. Please do it now or I'll have to call Mr. Sharrard."

Lucy ignored her and kept climbing.

At that point, I'm not going to lie, I was feeling pretty good about Lucy's bad choice. Maybe the day would turn out okay after all if she weren't part of it. "Look at that," I said to Nathan. "It only took, like, ten minutes and now she'll be hanging out with Mr. Sharrard for the rest of the day."

Mom stood there, her hands on her hips watching Lucy climb higher. In no time she was halfway to the top, trying to make her way through the thinner, shorter twigs, when—

"Whoa, whoa!" She made a grunting noise as the limb gave way. "Ow!" Lucy's body swung around and she was hanging upside down with her legs wrapped around a couple of branches. They were bending downward, and her hands were grabbing wildly for something to hold onto. "I need help!"

"Hang on, Lucy," Mom said calmly. "Don't move. I'm coming up."

I'd never seen my mom climb a tree before and even though this one was fake, she was doing a pretty good job. It took her three tries, but she was able to grab hold of the lowest branch and pull herself up.

I shook my head and said back at Nathan, "Check it out, my mom's actually up in a tr—"

He was gone. Little stabs of panic prickled through my body as I scanned down the shore. Nothing. I jogged up and down the grassy hillside. I looked behind the huge face. Nope. I squinted up the hill just in time to see Nathan's head disappear over the top, in the direction of the bright red posts of the mini-Golden Gate. *Of course,* I told myself, blowing out a relaxing breath of relief. The guy had been talking about it for weeks. I really didn't want to add to my mom's problems, but rule number one was to stay with your partner. I went after him.

I closed the distance pretty fast, but I was breathing hard, with beads of sweat breaking out on my forehead. It's not like I run up a lot of hills, especially while yelling at the same time. "Nathan!" I wheezed. "We need to stay together, man!"

I definitely didn't need this kind of drama. With Caryn around, the last thing I wanted was to rejoin our group with big dark spots blooming in my armpits. But what was I supposed to do, yell at Nathan for making me sweat?

He stood at the middle of the bridge, looking out at Puget Sound from the part of the sculpture that crossed over Western Avenue. I climbed up the bright red steps and walked toward him, trying my best to be casual.

"Dude, we've got to get back to our group." I stopped a few steps away. "How about if we check this out later?"

"Over two million vehicles have crossed the Golden Gate Bridge," Nathan mumbled while staring at his feet. "None have crossed this one, though."

It was one of his jokes. We both watched as the cars zoomed by on the four-lane street below us. "It's kind of funny that this thing is a sculpture and a real bridge, huh?" I said.

"Funny?" said Nathan. His nostrils flared out like he smelled something bad. "It's a useful way to connect the park where it's split by Western Avenue. So that's not funny. Interesting, maybe. Not funny."

Right, I thought, as my eyes feasted on Elliott Bay. It was such a beautiful place. I looked out across the Puget Sound to Alki Point, then beyond that to forested hills and islands, and finally the Olympic Mountains, hovering over it all like the biggest painting ever.

A few feet down from Nathan and me, an older man and woman looked out at the bay. The guy's t-shirt said "Seattle," with a big crease down the middle like he'd just bought it. The man nodded to us and said, "Shouldn't you fellas be in school?"

The lady chuckled and patted his shoulder, "Oh, stop it, Otto!"

"Actually, our class is on a field trip," I said, pointing toward the eraser. They're all down there by the—"

Then it happened.

4

It was the strangest thing. All these birds—like, the most I've ever seen—took off flying at the same time. From all over the place, the sky filled with black and white swirls, a million crows and seagulls squawking and cawing and drowning out everything. It felt like I was in the middle of a loud, weird dream.

That's when the hillside started moving—first rolling, then rippling like an ocean of dirt and grass. I was frozen, my brain totally unable to tell my body what to do. The bridge took care of that for me. It lurched sideways and threw me into the lady. We slammed our shoulders together and she went down on her side, making a grunting noise. I dropped to my knees from the shock of her bony body colliding with mine, and grabbed onto one of the support cables. The old man bent down to help his wife, then staggered and fell down next to her, clanging his head on something.

Nothing made sense, nothing looked normal. Down below, people were running in all directions. Mr. Sharrard and the chaperones chased after kids, trying to herd everyone together into an open space between sculptures. Most weren't paying attention and a few people were down on their stomachs. Finally, I could see Alex Blondino standing completely still in the middle of it all, screaming out the word that brought the truth crashing down on everyone:

"Earthquake!"

Nathan's hands were gripping the cable inches below mine. His eyes were squeezed shut and he was breathing hard.

"Hang on," I said, "It'll be okay."

The ground was still moving, which felt like riding a carousel, but one that was going sideways and diagonally and in circles all at once. Down the hill, Mr. Sharrard was stumbling around, still trying to gather up the stunned, terrified kids. People were falling, getting back up and falling again as the ground kept shifting underneath them. Some were trying to hold onto little bushes that were planted along a walkway. Sculptures swirled and shifted like trees in a storm. There was so much going on, I didn't even think to be scared until I remembered Mom. Was she still up in the fake tree with Lucy? I forced myself to focus through all the craziness and spotted her. She was still there, clinging to the bottom branch. There was no sign of Lucy.

"Mom!" I yelled, "I'm coming!"

She didn't hear me, so I just bolted. Getting off the bridge was a little rough, so I went slowly, grabbing one cable after the next. My knees and hips wobbled as I made my way off, zigzagging and slamming myself against the supports. A couple of times I fell onto the deck, close enough to see little bugs scrambling around the same way we all were. I finally made it to the steps and jumped off. My feet slid out from under me and my tailbone drove into the slope. A dull pain shot up my spine and into my head. I staggered to my feet and looked for Mom again, wondering if she'd seen me wipe out.

"Theo!" Mom mouthed as her palm shot out toward me. "Stay there!"

"But—"

I couldn't hear what she was saying but her finger jabbed at the air in my direction. That, combined with her intense glare could mean only one thing: to stay where I was. I crawled on my hands and knees back to the bridge steps and situated myself in a spot to ride things out. Just as I settled into a sturdy position, the creaking sounds started slowing down. At the same time, all the other noises— the screaming and yelling, the squeal of grinding metal—began to fade. Everywhere I looked, there were no birds to be seen or bird noises to be heard. Everything was still.

My butt, knees, shoulders and head ached from colliding with things and people. Slamming into the lady messed her up, too. When I climbed back onto the bridge, she was hunched over, blood dripping from her nose. She had a soaked red tissue pressed against her face, and already her brand new Seattle T-shirt was splotched with blood. The old guy stroked her hair as she cried. She tilted her chin up, which showed her white, tear-streaked face.

"Oh, Otto, what's happening?"

"Settle down, sweetie," said the man. "It was just a little earthquake. It's over now."

I looked back down the hill at Mom, who still seemed to be stuck in the fake tree. She was working to untangle herself from its spiky metal twigs. "Theo!" she yelled, "is everybody okay up there?"

The old man signaled in big motions like he was a kid waving down an ice cream truck. "My wife's a bit shaken up. It appears she may have broken her nose."

"Okay," said Mom. "Give me a minute to get out of this piece of art and I'll be right up there. There's a first aid kit on the bus." She eased herself out of the tree, constantly snagging her sweater. I could tell she was frustrated and she finally reached back and yanked hard on the orange material. *RRRRRip.*

"Perfect," Mom yelled. "My beautiful Angelou Elementary hoodie, ripped to shreds while stuck in a metal tree during an earthquake. Who'd have thunk it."

A little further away, Mr. Sharrard had assembled a group of kids by the face sculpture. He was counting as he patted each kid on the head. Other chaperones walked toward his group with more kids. And no sign of Lucy.

My eyes drifted back to the water. *Wow*, I thought. *A real earthquake.* I pulled my phone out and started filming, trying to make my voice sound like a news reporter. "This is Theo Cloverdale, coming to you from Olympic Sculpture Park, where an earthquake just took place." I aimed the camera at Nathan. "What do you think, Nathan?"

He was gazing out at the water. "Most likely between four and six on the Richter Scale."

"The what scale?" I aimed my phone up and down the waterfront, then pointed it at the Spaghetti Factory. Again, I kicked into my announcer voice.

"You're looking live at the world-famous Olde Spaghetti Factory." I zoomed in on the restaurant's red bricks and huge sign. "Excited for lunch— maybe I'll get spaghetti with meatba—"

It happened so fast my heart bounced.

A wall of white water shot up, framing every building along the shore with a curtain of spray. It arched over a building marked Pier 70, washed over the street and slammed into the Spaghetti Factory. Within seconds, the nearest street to the bay was flooded. Water came rushing in over the tracks and up the hill. Another wave pushed it in closer a few seconds later. Dirty foam started swallowing everything up—cars, trucks, signs—anything in its way.

Down at the tree sculpture, water was starting to slosh around the trunk just as Mom made it down to the lowest row of branches.

"Mom!" I screamed. "Go back up!"

"What?" she mouthed.

"Climb!" I stabbed the sky with my finger.

The water didn't stop rising. Mom's jeans ripped as she scrambled to get higher. I urged her on in my head. *Quickly! Higher! Keep going, Mom!* She shifted her body into a sitting position and balanced shakily on a couple of thin, wiry limbs. One of them snapped and she landed hard a couple rows down. She got a firm grip on a thicker branch, but now there wasn't more than a few inches between her and the brown, sloshing water. A torn piece of her sweater dipped into the muddy surge. Soon, only her head stuck above the water, but she was still trying to climb.

I was paralyzed. "Mom! Look out!"

A chunk of wood, maybe from a park bench, shot in out of nowhere and hit her in the back. Her head snapped forward—

—And she let go.

"Mom!"

Her arms flew out to her sides as our eyes met. Grabbing and slapping at the choppy froth of swirling garbage and other stuff, I could make out one word on her lips—

"Theo!"

I couldn't move. I tried, but how can you move when your heart decides to leave your body? A big, murky swell pushed her sideways and away from the tree, and just like that she was completely helpless inside the swirling water. She struggled to stay upright as she floated out, head darting side to side and arms grasping at anything she could use as a float. A tire brushed against her back and drifted away quickly. I kept watching, but only my eyeballs seemed able to function.

All down the Sculpture Park's hillside, people scrambled in all directions to avoid the water. Some weren't quick enough, and the water came at them like a shovel, scooping their feet out and dumping them butt-first into the swirl.

I spotted Caryn. A rush of warmth filled me when I saw her, but it would only last a blink. She stood on a bench, looking frantically for a way out, but the incoming surge was just too much. It knocked her backward and her feet shot out like so many other people I'd already seen. She slapped at the water as the fast-moving current dragged her quickly out past the railroad tracks. In an instant she vanished behind a pile of cars. "Caryn!" my dry voice squeaked. My head crackled with itchy electricity. The most horrifying, nightmarish movie was playing before my eyes.

But the pain and panic I felt told me I wasn't imagining anything. I found Mom again, but now she was a tiny speck in a sea of so many other specks. I yelled but there was no way she could've heard me. She'd stopped fighting the current and was floating further out. It became harder and harder to make her out among all the buildings and chunks of floating stuff. I didn't blink, didn't move, convinced that otherwise, I'd lose sight of her. It happened anyway. A second later, she just wasn't there anymore.

"No!" I screamed. I inhaled a glob of spit, coughing out in small, short chokes. A high-pitched, painful shriek filled the air. *Who's doing that?* It was me.

Up on the Golden Gate Bridge sculpture, me, Nathan and the old people, stood spread apart from each other, all of us gripping the side supports. Underneath, Western Avenue was a river framed by concrete banks that sloped down each side. Cars drifted and bounced against each other like plastic boats in a bathtub. More swells kept coming, and the hill below us started disappearing. Before I knew it, water was under us, in front of us, behind us. Nathan was shivering, his eyes squeezed shut. His hair stuck to his head from all the sweat and dirty water. To make things worse, the last wave had swamped over his shoes, which I could tell he didn't like at all.

"Take my hand," I said. "We'll go to the highest part of the bridge."

As he reached out to me, I heard Lucy's voice. She was in the water, coming right toward us. "Help! Glrrp! Help!" She was spinning in a swell, coming toward us fast. Her arms flapped like a crazy bird.

"This might be our only chance!" I yelled to Nathan. "When she gets close to you, grab her arm or leg or whatever you can! Understand?"

He knelt down and watched her as she bobbed closer.

"Nathan!" I yelled. "Grab her! Now!"

"How?"

"Reach through the cables!"

"Water's cold!"

"You can do this!"

He got on his stomach, dipping himself almost totally into the murky water and extending his arm between two bridge cables. Lucy lunged and missed, but Nathan was able to grab a piece of her jacket. Twirling around, she clutched his hand with her other arm. The water sloshed against them, loosening Nathan's grip, but his hand slid down her forearm and locked her fingers in his.

"Pull her in!" I shouted.

"Ahh! Cold!" he said, his hoodie strings completely submerged. He gave one big yank and pulled her close enough to reach the cable. We each took an arm and lifted Lucy up between the supports. She landed on her stomach, rolled to her side and hacked up a cloudy puddle of muck.

My heart pounded like a hammer inside my chest. "It's getting deeper!" I said. "We need to get to the highest part, where those old people are.!" The water was now so high that junk was crashing against the bridge, banging and clanging against the deck. We staggered up next to the couple who sat huddled together.

"We're trapped!" yelled Lucy. "I'm swimming for it!" She climbed between two cables and started lowering herself back into the brown foam.

"No!" I screamed, "You can't!" I held onto her arm. "You were lucky to make it back up here!"

"We're gonna die anyway!"

"Wait, look!" said the old guy, pointing to his feet.

I looked down. I could see my shoes. They were soaked, but the white rubber sparkled in the sun and wasn't submerged anymore. Patches of steel began peeking above the surface, and soon the whole bridge deck was visible, caked in gray sludge.

"It's going back out! Oh, my goodness, it is!" the old man shouted. He was laughing, crying, yanking his wife back and forth.

"Stop it, Otto!" she yelled. "My hip!"

"But we're okay, sweetie. We're going to be okay!"

Okay? I thought. *Nothing's okay, old man! Were you not standing right next to me watching my mom disappear?* I leaned against the rail, soaked and shivering. Everything around us was brown and a nasty smell filled the air, like rotten eggs. The odor grew thicker, burning the inside of my nose.

I was drained of the major surge of energy I'd had just minutes before. I blew out a long, deep breath and felt my arms drooping at my sides. Something fell out of my hand and clanged on the metal. My phone! It sat there in its waterproof case that Mom had bought me, teetering on the edge of plunging into the nasty-smelling soup below us. I scooped it up carefully, then stood and looked at the lit-up screen. My finger punched the "off" button.

No.

I'd just filmed everything.

5

Tears stung my eyes as I squinted down the shoreline. *I could've saved her and I froze.* I felt so cold, so empty. *I should've at least tried. Instead of swimming after her, I stood here and filmed it. Unbelievable.*

"Tsunami." Nathan's voice sounded as flat as someone ordering extra pickles with their Quarter Pounder.

"You mean, like, a tidal wave?" I said, cramming my phone into the front pocket of my damp jeans.

"Yes," he said. "Most likely caused by an earthquake along the Seattle Fault." He dug his knuckles into his ears and said, "The rift is a series of shallow east-west faults that cross the Puget Sound Lowland and pass under Seattle—"

"Well, time's a wastin'," the old guy blurted out. He groaned as he propped himself onto his knees and reached for a cable. "We ..." He tried to get up, but eventually just quit and plopped back down next to his wife. He cleared his throat and went to kiss her head but coughed into her hair instead. "We need to get to higher ground, and soon," he said, looking at me and Nathan.

Lucy's soaked sneakers made sucking noises as she walked up next to us. "This place is cursed. I'm not waiting around anymore."

"I like your attitude, young lady," the man said. "It seems appropriate that we introduce ourselves, seeing as we've just experienced all of this together." Extending his white, splotchy arm, he said, "I'm Otto, Otto James, and this is my wife, Sylvia." Otto patted her head lightly and extended his palm toward me. "And you are…"

"Theo Cloverdale," I said. I looked at the grandma-and-grandpa-looking couple through the haze in my brain. "And that's Nathan and Lucy."

"Cloverdale, now that's an interesting name. Indeed, it's a pleasure to meet all of you." Otto's quivering palm stuck out in my direction. "Would you good folks mind helping an old man up?"

I grabbed his hand and gave it my best shot, but Lucy had to join in before we were able to get him to his feet.

"Come on, Sylvia," he said, looking down at his wife. "Let's get out of here before we're trapped for good." He leaned down and tried to lift her by her armpits.

"Ahhh! Ohhh! Otto, my hip! Stop!"

"What's wrong with her?" said Lucy. "She sounds bad. She looks even worse."

Cracking and snapping noises were going on all around us. All down the waterfront, cars and trees and junk were scattered, piled on top of each other— some in little stacks, others in huge heaps. The Olde Spaghetti Factory sign was dark, no longer lit up in bright red letters like it had just been. Now, everything in sight had a gritty, brown coating. And down below, to make things a million times worse, no one in my class was around anymore.

But that wasn't all. We all seemed to see it at the same time. Down by the big eraser, in a puddle at the bottom of the hillside, something was bobbing up and down, slowly turning like a clock with one hand. I watched as a lady slid down the muddy slope toward it. Her hands covered her mouth as she splashed into the nasty muck, bent down and flipped it over. Actually, flipped *him* over.

It was a dead person.

I dropped down, propped my hands against my knees and gasped for air. I could hear Sylvia quietly sobbing and when I straightened up and looked at her, the area between her mouth and nose was covered in blood. She let out a wheezy, soundless scream. Then her body tensed up and she breathed in a huge gulp of air. "Ohhh, this is horrible! What's happening to us? It's a... a... a nightmare, Otto!" Bloody snot was pouring from her nose and her drool was thick and ropy between her teeth. It was gross but so much was going on, it didn't register all that much.

"Now, simmer down, Sylvia." Otto wiped her face with a soggy tissue. "We have to keep our wits about us, yes? Theo," he said, looking back at me. "Do you think you can give me a hand with Sylvia here?"

My head felt like a drawer already stuffed with too many socks, but more keep getting jammed in. "I need to find my mom," I said, swallowing back a fresh round of tears.

Otto raked away a damp strand of hair from his eye. "I understand that son, I really do, but if we keep moving we have a better chance of finding some help." His voice was shaky, and he kept licking his lips. He had to have been as cold and scared as the rest of us were.

"Okay," I said.

"Splendid. Now, get over to her other side. Gently put her arm around your neck and we'll lift her up. Try to relax, dear. Let Theo and me do the work."

Sylvia's body was stiff as a pole, and I almost dropped her.

"Agh! It hurts!" she wailed.

"Sorry, honey. Deep breaths, now," said Otto. "We'll be careful. Keep going Theo. That's right. See, she's very light."

Light? No way, I thought. She was like a big sack of rocks.

"Oh, it hurts too much! Don't make me stand!" Sylvia's knees folded again. "It just hurts... so... much." She cried in short little gulps.

"Honey, try not to put any weight on your legs," said Otto. "Just lean on Theo and me."

Everything we tried seemed to cause her extreme pain, so it took forever to get Sylvia in the right position for us to carry her, then another forever to get her off the bridge. Eventually, though, we'd made it to the highest part of the hill up next to the pavilion. Nothing was upright. Chairs, tables—everything was sideways or broken apart. Sylvia had groaned super loud in my ear several times, which was really annoying, so it was good to finally make it to some flat pavement and put her down. "This looks like a decent spot," Otto said. "It doesn't appear that the water made it this high."

There was a better view from this place. Other than the millions of little ponds and puddles all over the place, the water had returned to Elliott Bay. There was so much damage, it looked like a different planet, one that had a landscape of jagged chunks of muddy concrete and wood and trash. Loads of junk that didn't used to be junk—boats, streetlights, tipped-over cars—had just piled up in large or small clusters against whatever had kept them from being carried out to sea.

It was then that I learned to not look too hard at anything. Just a short way down, not far from where our bus was parked, another body was sprawled across the railroad tracks.

6

It was partly covered in wood and mud. Whoever the person was, their arms and legs were sticking out in weird ways. I could feel my brain begging my eyes to focus on something, anything, else.

But it wouldn't. *Is that Mom's body?* My heart instantly dropped until I realized that no, those weren't the clothes she was wearing. I tore my gaze away from the terrible scene and concentrated on carrying Sylvia. She was so limp and heavy, and I wasn't sure how much longer I could hold up my end.

"There, yes, right there," said Otto. He nodded toward a bench on the pavilion patio that incredibly was still standing on all four legs. Sylvia's groans were pretty much constant at this point. We laid her down as gently as we could on the bench. "Honey," said Otto, "I'm going to straighten out your legs."

"Ahhh! Ohhh!"

"There. All done. Just rest your head on my lap." Otto wedged himself under her and brushed her hair out of her eyes. "Just breathe, honey. It's going to be fine. Deep breaths, now." I watched his eyes as they stared out at the bay. "We'll just wait here until…" He sat up straight, pressing himself against the back of the bench and making Sylvia groan more. "Oh, no. No, please. Not again!"

I whipped my head around in time to see another wave slamming against the Edgewater Hotel, its spray covering it in a green, frothy crown. Twisty fingers of water snaked toward us, joining the little lakes from the first wave that hadn't washed back out. Next to the churning water, the sky looked as if it didn't belong, like it should be gray and stormy instead of sunny and blue.

"This one's coming in further," Nathan said, rubbing his ears with clenched fists.

The deck of the Golden Gate sculpture, where we'd just been a few minutes earlier, was already underwater. Only the spans stuck up above the swirling surges. The wave reached us, swamping our feet and ankles, re-soaking our pants. We were trapped, with our backs pinned against the pavilion wall.

"Look for something that floats!" yelled Otto over the noise. As the water crept up to my knees, I spotted something flat and white. It was about the size of a door and it was wedged up against a tipped-over dumpster.

"That?" I yelled, pointing to it.

"Yes, that!" Otto shouted. "Hurry! I'll help Sylvia up. Be quick, my boy!"

"Come on, Nathan!" I yelled, grabbing his arm. "Help me dig this thing out." The second I touched him I knew I shouldn't have.

"D-d-don't touch me!" He backed up a step.

I lurched backward. "Hey, man, sorry. Never mind." I sloshed over to it and dug out the foam slab, relieved that it was light after all that time I'd spent hauling Sylvia around. I floated it toward the rest of the group in the knee-deep water.

"Everyone grab on," said Otto. "We'll hold onto it like a raft." It was like standing around a floating dinner table, where each person had a place. The awful-smelling water was now to our waists and rising. Otto bear-hugged Sylvia, pinning her between him and our raft. The whole thing had to have looked super bizarre—two grown-ups and three kids playing Ring Around the Rosy in a big, dirty swimming pool. Slowly, we rose up and before long, my feet weren't touching the ground. It was freezing and my fingers were numb, but they still clamped onto the board with everything I had.

"Theo!" Otto gasped. He was struggling hard to keep him and Sylvia above water. His head kept going under and he'd come back up gasping for air. He went under again. "Paahh!" Otto spat out a fountain of spray when his head popped up. He went down again, using his body to keep Sylvia's head above water. I worked my way around the slab and eased Sylvia out of his grasp. I used all my strength to press her against the foam, enough to barely keep both of us above water. Otto's head shot back up, causing a major splash and throwing us all around while he flailed around for an open spot along the raft.

He found one next to Nathan and steadied himself. At that point, things improved. Sylvia must have gotten a burst of superhero strength, because she grabbed onto the foam board, let me go and started floating on her own. We were a more stable unit now as the surge pinned us against the pavilion wall and lifted us along it.

"Lucy! Look out!" I yelled. She was about to smack into a drainpipe. She dodged it a little but still bumped her head. For a second she looked stunned, but then she latched one arm onto the pipe and pulled on the board with the other, keeping us connected to the building.

Lucy was able to stabilize the raft, which was good because Sylvia was losing strength again. She started putting more of her weight on me, leaving my nose and mouth barely above the disgusting water. Inhaling some spray, I started choking and coughing from its salty, fishy taste.

"We're almost up to the roof!" yelled Otto. "Nathan, go around and grab the drainpipe. You can hold it while Lucy climbs up top!"

Nathan worked his way around to Lucy, clinging to my back and dunking me a little. He found a good grip on the post and the raft, and Lucy turned her attention to getting to the roof.

At the top of the next surge she gave a huge kick. Her soaked sneaker curled over the top of the gutter while her fingers clawed for a grip. Then she vaulted herself sideways and onto the roof.

Nathan was also starting to wear out. His head was barely above the water, still trying to keep a grip on the pipe and the raft. Lucy got on her stomach and held onto our float, allowing Nathan to let go and cling to the drainpipe with both arms. I pushed while Lucy pulled Nathan up, then him and Lucy lifted me out.

We still had to somehow get Otto and Sylvia out of the water. Otto rotated the float so that Sylvia was directly below Lucy. "Pull her up!" he spat. Each of Lucy's yanks made Sylvia scream like she was being stabbed with a sword, so I took one side and Lucy took the other and we lifted Sylvia up by the armpits. She still groaned a lot, but the three of us were eventually able to get both her and Otto up on the roof.

"We need to move to as high as possible," said Otto. "See how the roof slopes up to the east?"

My body burned and my fingers were cramping into claws from gripping everything so hard. "Can we rest for a second?" I said.

"No!" Otto barked. A fold of skin quivered under his chin.

"Okay!" I snapped.

"I'm sorry," said Otto, sniffing. "I understand, we've all been through a lot. But I think we need to move to the highest point of the roof, and as soon as possible."

"Obviously," said Lucy, retying one of her shoes. "Thanks for the mansplanation."

We lifted Sylvia again, half carrying, half dragging her along the roof Finally, Otto said, "This is as high as it goes." We laid her down and she started shivering, so hard you could hear her teeth clacking. Otto hugged her tight and rubbed her back, but it wasn't keeping her from shaking. Her skin was the color of a new sidewalk.

I scanned the shoreline. "Water's going back out," I said.

"So what?" said Lucy. "Now, we're stuck on this stupid roof. How are we supposed to get off?" She sat down and flipped back her soaked, muddy hair. "I knew I should've swam for it a long time ago."

"We had no choice," Otto said. "There was nowhere else to go. We'll have to stay up here until help comes. It can't be long."

But it was— a soaked, frozen, long time. We sat and shivered, bunched together like a football huddle. The big waves had stopped coming in, and now it was hard to tell if they were new surges or just water sloshing around, looking for a place to settle.

My thoughts were fuzzy, but my eyes couldn't stop searching down the waterfront, as if I could somehow spot Mom among all the billions of things that looked out of place. Nothing made sense. Nothing was normal.

Quietly at first, the sounds of sirens filled the air. I looked at Otto. His bloodshot eyes seemed like they were about to pop out of his skull. "Sirens!" he shouted. "What a beautiful sound! We're rescued! Ha! Ha! Hallelujah!"

Lucy sprung to her feet. "You're happy to hear the cops coming? Whatever. Now I'm totally out of here."

"Wait," said Otto, waving a finger at Lucy. "You can't just jump off the roof! What's your name, little girl?"

She slapped the air above his hand. "Don't point at me, old man. And I'm not a little girl."

"Her name's Lucy," said Nathan, arms bear-hugging his knees.

"Lucy," said Otto, "those aren't police sirens, they're fire engines. And they're here to help."

For a quick second, reality evaporated from my thoughts. *What a relief! We're saved! Mom's going to be so happy to know that I'm okay. Oh, wait...*the truth whacked me in the face and a gusher of tears poured out.

"It's going to be okay, Theo." I felt Otto's shaky grip on my shoulder. "They'll find your mom. Hey… listen… helicopters!"

My eyes followed the new sound as it grew louder. Four red helicopters appeared out of nowhere and shot out over the water.

"See what I mean?" Otto said. "They're sending out the cavalry."

I felt a tiny point of warmth inside me. They might find her after all. Maybe they even already did.

Mom might be okay.

7

The sirens kept getting louder and soon a fire truck pulled up below us. It had a giant ladder and a driver in the back. "Over here!" yelled Otto. They could definitely see us, but Otto was again waving his arms, as if they might not notice that we were right above them.

Firefighters sprung from the truck and the big ladder started rotating our way. When it touched the roof, two firefighters climbed up, hauling large tool boxes with them. A couple more followed with axes and other big tools. They worked like a machine. One of them headed for Otto and Sylvia. Another other came up to me and Nathan, knelt down and raised his face shield.

"Hey guys, my name's Jerome."

"Hey," I said.

"You look pretty cold. Let's get you some blankets." He opened his backpack and pulled out stacks of folded silver sheets. "See, you just unfold it... like this." He handed it to Nathan. "These things keep you warmer than you'd think. Wrap these around you, and I'm just gonna check you out real quick to make sure no one needs urgent medical attention." He opened his kit and pulled out a stethoscope. "Did either of you hit your head?"

"No," I said. Thoughts of my mom slammed into me, causing a panic that choked off my voice. "Are you looking for my mom?"

"What's your name, boss?" said Jerome.

"Theo."

"If you can just hang tight, Theo," said Jerome, pointing a light in my eyes, "we can get to that in just a second—"

"Why?" I pointed at the water. "She's out there. Right now."

"Got it. Now if you can just slow down—"

"She fell out of a tree. She floated away!"

Jerome's eyes locked with mine as he strapped a black cuff around my arm. "When did she float away?"

"I don't know, like, a few hours ago."

"Blood pressure's normal." He pulled off the cuff. "Okay, if she's only been out there for an hour, there's a good chance we'll find her. There's already boats and 'copters all over the place."

Hearing the confidence in Jerome's voice made me feel another small sparkle of hope. I sucked in a couple of deep breaths to keep from losing it. *She might be safe, somewhere waiting for me,* I thought. *But she might not be, either.*

"What's your name, man?" Jerome said as he turned to Nathan. The sudden attention made Nathan flinch.

"Nathan," he said, barely above a whisper.

"What's up, Nathan. Feelin' okay?"

He didn't answer.

"Nathan," I said. "Do you feel okay?"

"Yes."

I hadn't paid any attention to where Lucy was until I spotted her down by the ladder truck. She must have climbed down the ladder to the ground without anyone noticing, because now she was touching everything on the truck and crawling all over it.

"Do we get to ride on this thing?" she yelled.

"Probably not," shouted Jerome, turning to look at her. "And your name is—?"

"Lucy!"

My guts churned listening to Lucy saying her own name in her annoying Lucy voice. I think in that moment I hated her more than I'd ever hated anyone. She was the whole reason Mom climbed that metal tree and got stuck. If that stupid jerk could've just followed the rules, Mom would probably be here right now. Instead—I couldn't hold it in anymore. "Shut up, Lucy!"

"Whoa," said Jerome. "She's allowed to tell me her name, Theo. Relax."

Relax? Really? I was so mad my lips were quivering. "If my mom wasn't chasing her around, she would've lived. It's all her fault!"

Lucy climbed around the back of the truck and out of sight.

"Listen, man," Jerome said, "first of all, your mom isn't dead. She's missing. Those are two completely different things. And second, you can't blame Lucy for this. She didn't cause that tidal wave." He closed his box and looked down at her. "Lucy! Off the rig! The last thing we need is to have to treat you for a broken leg!"

Lucy jumped off the firetruck and landed hard on the pavement, slamming down on her side. "Oof! I'm okay!"

"Is she always that energetic?" Jerome asked.

"Yeah," I said. "Yeah, she is." I heard another siren and saw an aid car stopping in front of the fire truck. "Is that for Sylvia?"

"It's for everybody. You're all getting a ride up to Harborview. You need to be checked by a doctor just to make sure and then..."

"Wait, what? No!" I said. "I can't leave!" A hot knot immediately started swelling in my throat. *Don't cry,* I urged myself. I had to be respectful, reasonable. "She's out there somewhere, and I can't leave." I slowed my words down even more to sound as calm as I possibly could. "I'm fine. I can stay here. You're done checking me, right?"

"Yep," Jerome said. "But we still need to get you all out of here. Being on the roof of a building in the middle of a tsunami zone is fairly high-risk."

I got to my feet, peeling my damp butt from the pavilion roof. Feeling dizzy, my knees folded. Little sparkles swam around in front of my eyes, so I crouched down, letting the blood fill my head and focusing on the far-off Olympic Mountains. They looked the same as always, but so much of the view beneath them had changed. The dizziness passed and I stood back up. "Okay," I said. "Anyway, I'm just gonna head down the shore and look around. I can get myself down the ladder. I'll see you later."

"Dude, listen," Jerome reached out his hand to block my way. "Hundreds of other people are looking for your mom." His forearm was beefy, and a blue tattoo wrapped around his bicep. "We're in a danger zone here. Another wave could hit and make our day a lot worse than it is right now."

"But the waves have stopped!" A fresh well of tears was about half an inch behind my eyes and ready to blow. "I've been watching. It's... it's been totally calm."

"I understand," said Jerome, "but let's get off this roof. I'll help you down while Michelle and Trevor get Sylvia into a rescue sled." He climbed down a couple of rungs and stopped. "Okay, take it slow. I'll be right behind you. Leg, hand, leg, hand. Perfect."

Once me and Nathan were on the ground, we watched as the firefighters on the roof attached a rope to Sylvia's stretcher and to the ladder. They carefully balanced her on the top rung, making sure she stayed level while they tilted the ladder downward. Jerome held a rope from ground level to keep everything steady while they gently lowered her. After she was safe at the bottom, Jerome jogged over and opened the back doors of the EMT vehicle. "Hop in, guys. Let's go, Lucy!"

Nathan climbed in first and slid down the long seat. I stepped in and sat next to him. It smelled like a doctor clinic. Lucy jumped inside, working her way to the back and messing with everything in her reach. All I could do was stare at her and silently rage. She was only good at one thing: making everyone around her miserable.

They put in Sylvia, then Otto and Jerome climbed in and that was everybody.

"How'd you get her off the roof so fast?" said Lucy, playing with a roll of blue tape.

"Lots of practice," Jerome said as we started moving.

"Wait!" I yelled, making Nathan jerk. "Let's just look one more time. Maybe my mom's trying to come up the hill right now." I stood up and smacked my head hard on something. It hurt so bad I couldn't see for a second.

"Theo," Jerome said, "sit down and try to relax. I know this is hard, but..."

"You don't know!" I yelled, rubbing my head. "How would you know?"

Things got quiet and I leaned over, putting my head in my hands. I felt like such a coward. Mom never would've left me. Her face flashed into my head, and the look it had the second she fell in the water—surprised for a second, then looking all around for a way out. She was a fighter. Unlike me.

Otto's voice broke the silence. "Jerome, was that a real tsunami?"

"That's what they're saying." A voice crackled in his radio. "Hang on, I've got to get this... Fast Response Unit Four Seven Seven, go ahead." He put the device to his ear. I could make out an unclear, scratchy voice on the other end.

"Stand by," Jerome said. His eyes found me. "Theo, is your last name Cloverdale?"

"Y-yes." My heart plunged like a rock kicked off a cliff.

Jerome dipped his head. "That's affirmative. He's on board and in transit." He nodded. "Yes. Copy... will do. Out." Jerome slid the radio back on his belt. "Theo, that was the Seattle Police. When we get to the hospital, they want to talk to you."

"About what?"
Jerome cleared his throat and looked at me.
"About your mom."

8

"What about her?" It felt like I might barf.

Jerome scooted around and put his hand on my shoulder. "Listen, man—they just want to ask you some questions, to help them find her."

I knew I should've stayed at the waterfront, showing the rescue teams where everything happened. I dug my fingertips into my eyes, which were dry and gritty.

"Theo, I need to tell you something," Otto said. He sat by Sylvia's head, stroking her hair like he'd been doing on and off all day. "You were brave today. Courageous. And you, too, Lucy and Nathan." He nodded his wrinkly forehead toward them. "We're not going to forget what you did, helping us out of that jam. Isn't that right, honey?"

Sylvia had a bag of clear liquid hooked up to her arm and when she looked at me, her eyelids drooped so much I could barely see her eyeballs. "Yesss, yess, thank you so much, sweeties." Her leg was wrapped in something that looked like a big water wing.

Suddenly my seat was shaking like crazy. When I looked over, Lucy was shivering so hard I could hear her teeth slamming together.

Jerome pulled a blanket out and put it over her shoulders. "Here, let's get you warmed up."

She hugged herself tightly, mumbled something, then shouted, "We could've died! We could have died! We're gonna die! We're—gonna d—"

"Stop!" Nathan was hunched over, rocking back and forth, his hands cupped over his ears. "Stop it!"

Things were falling apart fast. "It's okay, man," I said, lightly placing my hand on his shoulder.

Jerome hopped up next to Lucy. He pulled a clear mask out of somewhere and gently put it over her face. "Here, Lucy. Just a little oxygen. Breathe slowly. There you go."

"I want my mom," said Nathan. It sounded all muffled with his face pressed against his wet jeans.

"You'll see her soon." I said. I tried to remember how Susan, his mom, would help him when he was overloaded. "Just breathe... in... and out... and in..."

Gradually he lifted his head, straightened up and looked toward the back window of the ambulance. "The tsunami may have flooded the Duwamish River too. It possibly even struck as far south as Commencement Bay." He was back.

I looked at Jerome. "He's pretty smart."

Jerome studied the digital image as he took Sylvia's blood pressure. "I can tell."

Before long, the siren switched off and we came to a stop. The back doors opened and a guy in blue hospital scrubs ducked his head in. "Hi, I'm Matt. I'm a nurse." He pointed at Sylvia. "She's first, then you all can hop out."

Matt and Jerome slid Sylvia's gurney out onto the pavement, and she disappeared into an ocean of scrub-wearing hospital people. Jerome and Matt leaned their heads back in. "Let's go, friends," said Matt. "We'll try to make your stay as short as possible."

Lucy grabbed onto the back of her seat. "I'm not going in there!" she yelled, "And you can't make me!"

Of course, I thought, my guts boiling. Nothing was ever easy with her.

Even Jerome rolled his eyes a little. "Theo, how about you go first and show Lucy that this is no big deal. Lucy, no one's going to hurt you."

"I don't even know you." Lucy held out her hand. "Give me twenty bucks and I'll come out."

Jerome pulled out his wallet. "Here's ten."

Really? I thought. Lucy grabbed the money and shoved her way past me, slamming my elbow into an oxygen tank.

Outside, it was quite a scene. I'd never seen that many people wearing all plastic, from hats down to shoe covers. "Follow me, guys," said Matt. "We'll find a place for you inside."

As always, Nathan tailed me so close I could feel his clammy breath on the back of my neck. When I stopped, he slammed into me. "Dude, a little space please? You aren't going to lose me, okay?" He just blinked a few times, which is what he usually does when I try to correct him. The ER doors swooshed open, and we weaved our way through all the people and chairs and equipment. We followed Matt down a hallway lined with wheeled beds and into a small exam room.

"Hang tight," said Matt. "Shouldn't be long until a doctor comes by." He yanked a curtain closed and disappeared.

Nathan backed a chair up against the curtain and sat hunched over, staring at the floor. I climbed up on the exam table and took a long, deep breath. The more my body relaxed, the more my brain started taking over. Different scenes from the morning played out of order—the cars slamming against each other right underneath us, the birds taking off, Nathan helping Lucy—

"You saved Lucy," I blurted out.

"What?" said Nathan.

"Back at the bridge, you pulled her out of the water. You saved her."

He started rubbing his eyes. "She grabbed my hand."

"Yeah, but you reached your hand out to her. Even though the water was cold, and it was dangerous, you still did it."

Nathan squinted and rubbed his hands together—fast, faster.

He's stressing, I thought. I needed to change the subject, but I couldn't think of anything to say, so I just kept my mouth shut and watched Nathan rock in the plastic chair until he slowed down and finally stopped. As I retreated back into my own head and stretched out on the exam table, I couldn't stop thinking about Mom. All the would-haves and should-haves ate away at my mind until the swelling throat lump started choking me again. I remembered what Jerome had said, that there was a chance. With my head resting on the paper pillow, I closed my eyes and lost myself inside my brain.

I thought about how Mom had always been so strong, especially since Dad left. Whatever it took to make sure I had clothes and food and just someone there to listen to my problems, she was good for it every time. I missed her so much it hurt to breathe.

"Get away from me! I don't need a stupid doctor!" Lucy's voice invaded the swirling nightmare in my head. She was somewhere on the other side of the curtain, and she must've been pretty close.

The woman's voice was calm. "Lucy, is there someone we can call? A family member?"

Lucy's voice got a little softer. "My sister. She's an adult. Almost."

"Okay, perfect. Do you mind giving me her number?"

"I don't know her number. It's on my phone." I could hear Lucy struggling to pull it out of her wet jeans.

"Stupid thing is dead," she said. "Hey, Theo!" The curtain between us jerked open. "Let me use your phone. I need to call my sister."

"How'd you know I was in here?" I said. I could smell Lucy as she came closer, adding her fishy seawater aroma to me and Nathan's fishy seawater aromas.

"I came in right behind you." She showed me the folded-up bill between her fingers. "With my new ten bucks." Next to her was a woman in a sweater, jeans and boots. Her shoulder-length hair was white.

"Hi," the lady said. "I was going to come over and talk to you two next. My name is Julie. I'm a social worker. My job is to help you get reconnected with your families."

"My mom's available," said Nathan, "but Theo's isn't."

Ouch. I knew he wasn't trying to be mean, but his honesty could be brutal sometimes.

"Theo," Julie said. "I've been trying to call and text your dad, but he hasn't replied."

"Yeah, that kind of sounds like him," I said, reaching for the bulky phone case in my front pocket. I pried it out, pressed the power and it came right on. 22 percent power. "I don't see my dad very m—" Before I knew it, my phone was in Lucy's hand. "Hey!" I said.

Her face lit up in the phone's glow as she texted her sister. *So much for not knowing her number,* I thought.

"She's at work," said Lucy, her voice a little bit calmer. "She gets off at ten."

Julie put her notebook on the counter and looked at Lucy. "I can talk to her manager. She can come right now—"

"It's not that easy!" Lucy yelled. "She takes the bus. Can you pick her up, Julie?"

We all stood there and had another uncomfortable moment, thanks to Lucy. Like always, no one knew what to say. Adults didn't know her like us fifth graders did. We were used to Lucy's disrespect. We all knew how much she loved to throw people off, or even better yet, shock them.

Even so, her behavior there in the hospital wasn't nearly as shocking as it was that one day at show-and-tell.

9

You know how sometimes you just like to do kid stuff—fun things you used to like doing when you were little? Maybe it could be watching Little Mermaid or playing in a ball pit—just random stuff that reminds you of when you were young and clueless, but happy.

I think that's why, when Mr. Sharrard asked us to choose a fun afternoon activity, Room 302 voted to have a show-and-tell. No other ideas even came close, so that's exactly what we did one Friday.

"Kenny," said Mr. Sharrard, "thank you for sharing your collection of animal skins with us. You might want to tell your folks there's some water damage to that bag of tails." He patted Kenny's shoulder and aimed him back toward his desk. "And you're sure one of those isn't my uncle's missing hair piece?"

"Henh," Nathan giggled behind me.

"Okay, who's next?" Mr. Sharrard asked, his eyes peeking at us from above his reading glasses.

Lucy's arm shot up.

"Yes, Lucy. Step right up," Mr. Sharrard said. "Glad you're sharing today. What have you got for us?"

She scooted her chair out, unzipped her backpack and pulled out a folded-up piece of paper. She walked slowly up the far aisle, working her way to the front of the class. Stopping and unfolding the paper, she held it out in front of her face.

It was a printout of a guy sitting on a picnic table, smiling.

"This is my dad," she said, poking her head around the page. "It's the only picture I have of him."

She shuffled sideways from one side of the room to the other, like she wanted everybody to get a real good look. In the photo, the man's arms looked thin but muscular, sticking out of a yellow t-shirt that said *Maui 2008* in cracked, red letters. His eyes were the same as Lucy's—big and so dark they were almost black. And his smile—it was that same look she'd get just before acting up.

Mr. Sharrard cleared his throat. "I indeed see a family resemblance. Nice-looking chap, your father."

She stopped pacing and planted herself front and center, sticking the picture out as far as her arms could stretch. It shook a little, she gripped it so tight.

"Well, thank you then, Lucy," said Mr. Sharrard, making his way up to the front. "If that's everything you wanted to share, go ahead and pick the next person to—"

Rrrip. She tore the picture of her dad in half, right down the center.

"He's dead," Lucy said with a blank expression on her face.

"Whoa!" I could hear whispers from all over the room.

Her eyes locked in on each of our shocked faces, one at a time. Scanning the classroom again, she stomped over by the door and let the paper slip through her fingers and into the recycle bin. Then she ran back to her seat and put her head down.

No one seemed to know what to say, even Mr. Sharrard.

****

A white-coated lady swooped into our exam room. "Hi guys, I'm Dr. Kumasaka." She pulled the curtain shut to separate me and Nathan from Lucy and Julie, then sat down and looked at her laptop. She glanced at us, then put a stethoscope to her ears. "I'm just going to give you two a quick once-over to be on the safe side."

Again? I thought. I was tired of people poking at me. My body felt fine.

"Let's take a look at you first, Theo," she said. "Go ahead and sit up." As I did, I noticed a poster on the wall behind the doctor. It had illustrations of male and female bodies. No skin, just muscles and organs and nerves.

"If you don't mind, Theo, I'm going to lift up your shirt a little, here... your clothes are soaking," said Dr. Kumasaka. "We'll get you two some dry scrubs to put on ASAP. Okay, go ahead and sit up." She started shining her light at my mouth, then ears, then nose...

Again, the curtain flew open and with it, the sound of another familiar voice. "Oh! My baby! Oh, thank goodness!" It was Susan, Nathan's mom. "Baby, I'm so glad you're safe!" She darted toward him and swallowed up his body, her face buried in his hair. His hand popped out and grabbed the sleeve of her shirt.

"Hi, Mom." Nathan's voice was muffled. Susan rocked him back and forth, like a baby. It was good to see—but made my heart sting thinking about my mom.

"Theo! Oh, honey!" Susan let go of Nathan and sprang at me. I'm sure she was trying to be nice, but I was definitely not comfortable with her hugging me while the doctor had my shirt pulled up to my armpits. Her face looked like she'd just been punched. "Sweetie," she squeaked, pulling my face into her coat and patting me each time a word came out, "I-am-so-sorry." She sniffed and put her hands on my cheeks. "They're going to find her. You know that, right?"

"Theo," said Dr. Kumasaka, pulling my shirt back down, "do you have a way to get back home?"

Susan's watery eyes stared into mine. "He can come with us," she sniffed. "We'll make room. Theo, you can stay with us as long as you'd like."

I suppose I should've felt grateful for Susan's generous offer, but the thought of living with her and Nathan—and his baby sister Becky—just really hit me like a slap to the face. It meant I wouldn't be going home.

The doctor smiled at Susan. "Are you an emergency contact?"

"I am, yes," said Susan, holding out a sheet of paper. "Right there, top of the list." She looked at me and her face transformed back to the pained look. "I'm also his mom's best... best fr... I'm sorry." She fished a used tissue out of her purse. "We're like family."

Dr. Kumasaka quickly finished examining Nathan and opened the curtain, revealing Lucy again. She was sitting in a chair, her arms folded and her body facing away from Julie. Julie patted Lucy a couple of times, got up and came into our room. "Just so you know," she said, facing Susan, "we did try to contact Theo's father, but got no reply."

"Not a surprise," Susan said coldly.

My dad had a reputation for being undependable. There had been a couple of times after he'd moved out when he said he was going to take me out to ice cream or a baseball game or something, and he just didn't show up.

"Okay, you guys are good to go." The doctor wrote something down on a card and gave it to Susan. "They're both fine—physically, anyway. Keep an eye on 'em and call me if you have questions about anything at all. I would also suggest making an appointment with a pediatrician. These guys have had a very tough day, and it might help for them to talk to someone about it."

"I'll do that." Susan took the card. "Thank you, Dr. Kumasaka."

"Of course. Now, everyone, go home and get some rest, doctor's orders." Her eyes were glued to her laptop as she sprung up and stepped around the curtain. I could hear the squeak of shoes on the Emergency

Room floor.

"Oh, I'm sorry," Dr. Kumasaka said. "I need to watch where I'm going."

"No worries, Doctor," said a different voice. For a split second, I thought my mom's face would be the one belonging to it. She'd peek in and say "Yoo hoo," or something dorky, but we'd be so happy to see each other. I'd tell her to stop climbing fake trees and we'd laugh a whole lot and I'd hug her tighter than I've ever hugged anybody, and we'd leave this scary hospital forever.

Of course, it wasn't her. The lady who came in was smaller than Mom, and super fit. Her black braid went down past the collar of her Seattle cop shirt. "Hi guys, …"

"The X-26 Taser has two spare cartridges." Nathan was sitting up straight. When she looked at him, he turned his head away.

"Sounds like you know a little bit about law enforcement tools. I'm Sergeant Loden." She pulled out a little note pad. "And you two are Theo and Nathan, correct?"

We nodded and she lowered herself onto the rolling stool. Her clothes looked really uncomfortable—a belt with a bunch of stuff on it and a bullet-proof vest that was digging into her ribs.

"If you don't mind," she said, "I'd like to hear what happened today. Who wants to go first?"

The sergeant was nice and everything, but the last thing I wanted was to go over it all again. "I guess I can," I said, then told her everything I could remember, which took quite a while.

"Okay, last question, Theo," she said. "What time did you last see your mom?"

Hmm, I thought. I was definitely hungry at the time, especially after getting that whiff of Spaghetti Factory in the air. "Um, I think it was around 10:00 or 10:30."

"Tell me what was going on."

My brain felt scrambled. "She was being pulled out by the current. It was so strong. I guess the last place I saw her was down by the train tracks. She tried to grab a pole... but it didn't work, then she floated behind the Spaghetti Factory, and, um, that was the last..." I couldn't get another word out and started crying, this time without the usual throat lump as a warning. I snorted and snuffed, using the back of my hand to keep the tears and snot from running down my face.

Sergeant Loden wheeled to the counter, reached around Nathan and pulled out a couple of tissues. She placed them in my hand, squeezing my shoulder as she stood up. "Try not to lose hope, my friend. I know you might think that the odds are stacked against your mom, but we've been finding people—alive—in some crazy places."

"But...?" I said, honking hard into a tissue, "what about everybody else that was there? And Mr. Sharrard?" I sounded whiny. I needed to get it together.

"I'll do some checking on that," said Sergeant Loden, "and I promise that I'll tell you guys everything I know as soon as I know it, okay? It's the least I can do for such brave young men and women." The sergeant stood up. "Julie and I will work together to keep you updated."

"Okay," I said. Julie looked at me with a faint smile.

"And here's something else to think about, Mr. Theo." The sergeant hooked her thumbs around her big police belt. "Right now, as we speak, the Coast Guard and every search and rescue unit in western Washington is out there looking for your mom and your class." She hitched up her vest. "These people are trained for these types of things. Help will get to her and everyone down there."

I suddenly shivered with the thought: *Down where? By the water... or under it?*

"Here's my card," she said. I took it with the hand that wasn't already crammed with soggy tissues. I sniffed hard and slid off the exam table. I looked across at Lucy, who was talking to Julie.

"My sister said she can get me at eight. I'll just hang out in the waiting room or whatever." Her eyes met mine. "What are you looking at?"

"Julie," said Susan, "can I speak with you in the hallway, please?"

As soon as they left the room, a woman brought in hospital scrubs for us to change into. She didn't seem to notice Lucy going through the drawers and stuffing Band-Aids and cotton swabs into her pockets. "I guess we won't have to worry about going to school for a while," Lucy said, tossing my phone back. "School's dumb, anyway."

Susan came back in and smiled at Lucy. "Lucy, we can give you a ride home."

"Fine," Lucy said.

Lucy's disrespectful voice made my jaws tight. *Maybe try being grateful every once in a while,* I thought. After changing and stuffing our wet clothes into plastic bags, we followed Susan out of the bustling ER. I tried not to look around too much, but it was impossible. People were all over the place, some right in the middle of the hallway or slumped against the wall, covered in blankets. A few were laying down, hooked up to bags of liquid like Sylvia and some were just sitting on the floor zoning out. As I scanned the packed lobby, I realized we all had one thing in common on that sunny day:

We were all wet.

10

"Guys," said Susan as she pushed the elevator button for the parking garage, "we need to swing by daycare to pick up Becky on our way home."

I climbed into the back of Susan's car and crammed myself in next to the baby seat, which was planted in the middle. Little kid garbage was everywhere—crushed goldfish, fruit roll-up wrappers, little pieces of carrot or stuff that looked like carrots. Digging around for the seatbelt, I could feel crumbs wedging themselves under my fingernails.

Nathan sat up front, staring straight ahead as the car wound its way out of the parking garage. My view of Lucy was blocked by the baby seat, and before long, she'd gotten so quiet that I almost forgot she was there.

I leaned back and tried to relax a little as my eyes locked onto a brown smudge on the ceiling of the car. It made me think of Nathan and Susan and Becky's messy apartment and that I wouldn't be going home. Instantly, tears stormed in, begging to be let go. I cried quietly, keeping my mouth shut and looking out the window. The last thing I wanted was for Lucy, who was just inches away from me, to notice and mock me about it.

The idea of staying at Nathan's was so frustrating. I should've at least been able to stay where all my stuff was, a place where I didn't have to worry about sitting on half-eaten granola bars and dealing with babies.

As we headed out of downtown Seattle, things looked pretty much the same as always—at first. People were still walking around, traffic lights still worked. But once we got to the highest point of the West Seattle Bridge, I could tell something big was going on out over Elliott Bay.

"Whoa," I said, rubbing my eyes. Ships and boats packed the bay and helicopters hovered low over the water, moving in tight circles.

"Sergeant Loden was right," said Susan, looking into her rear view mirror. "They *are* all over this."

Maybe, I thought. But it was starting to get dark, and then it would be a lot easier for someone to be invisible. The further away we got from the water, the more desperate I felt. As we drove up the hill into West Seattle, I couldn't keep a lid on it anymore. "Susan, can you take me back? Back down there?"

"Theo—"

"Susan, I can help. I can tell them what I saw, and we can look for her." Just saying the word "her" created another throat lump that choked off my voice.

"Shut up, you little baby." Lucy's eyes had nothing but poison in them when she poked her head out from the other side of Becky's car seat.

"You shut up, Lucy!"

"That's enough! Both of you!" Susan yanked the wheel sideways and pulled the car over in the parking lot of Taco Time. She threw her arm over her seat and glared at us. Then her eyes got softer.

"Theo, I'm so sorry, but we can't go down there. The streets are blocked off and only first responders are allowed in." Her palm brushed the back of my head. "And that's a good thing, honey. Remember what the sergeant told us? They're doing everything humanly possible to find your mom." She turned back around and ruffled Nathan's hair. "Let's go home, guys."

We picked up Becky at Little Pilgrims Daycare, then stopped at Wendy's drive-through. Becky sat between me and Lucy. Her nose really needed a good wiping, and she was just sitting there staring at me. Susan pulled the take-out bags through the window into the car. My stomach gurgled at the aroma of French fries, and I remembered that I hadn't eaten since breakfast. Seemed like a week ago.

"Fries, Mommy!" Becky's grubby little fingers stuck out as she reached toward the bag.

"When we get home, Becky Bug."

"Fries now!" Saying the "f" sound made soggy goldfish specks spray out of her mouth.

Then, all of a sudden, the food didn't smell so good. I felt hot and dizzy, like there just wasn't enough air in their stuffy car. Cold sweat rolled down my neck and my mouth filled up with spit. I rolled down the window and stuck my head out, taking a long, deep breath of cool night air. *Ahhh. Better.* The wind slapped at my face and slowly sucked most of the sick out of me.

"Everything okay, Theo?" Susan said.

"Yeah," I said. As the breeze dried the tear streaks and sweat from my face, I wondered what had happened to my lunch. Was it still on the bus? Did it fly out a window and get washed away? Eaten by a seagull? What about the bus? Sunk to the bottom? Did Mom sink too? The thought made me want to scream into the wind, and I kept my head sticking out the window like a dog all the way down Delridge Way. Every once in a while, I'd feel Becky's little fingers tugging on my sleeve but I didn't pay attention. As long as Susan didn't care, things were just fine the way they were.

I started seeing familiar stuff—Safeway, the library—and felt good enough to bring my head back inside the car. Lucy was giving Susan directions to her apartment. "See that place up there on the right? Yep, right there—Highland Court. You can just drop me off in front."

"Oh, that's okay," said Susan, pulling in behind a dented Subaru wagon. "We can walk you in."

"Whatever."

Lucy bolted out the door and we all hurried to catch up, following her up the stairs and into a long hallway that smelled bad, like vegetable soup left on the stove too long. She stopped at apartment 217, all the way down on the left. "This is it," Lucy said, pounding the door. She knocked some more. Then some more. When it opened, a hot blast of burnt oven odor and dirty laundry blew into our faces. Something else, too—maybe cinnamon?

"Hi." The girl in the doorway smiled, holding a plate stacked with buttery cinnamon toast. "Want some?" She looked like an older version of Lucy, with orange hair and a nose ring.

"No thanks. Looks good, though." Susan put out her hand. I'm Susan."

"I'm Steffie."

"And I'm out of here." Lucy pushed through their handshake, brushing against Becky's little feet and out of sight. As she disappeared, a whiff of cigarette smoke hit my nose, and a dude popped in next to Steffie. He squinted as the cigarette bounced in his mouth.

"'Sup." He blew a blue cloud out of the side of his mouth and vanished behind the half-open door.

"That's Chad," Steffie said as she started closing the door. "Thanks for bringing her home."

Susan shifted Becky to her other side and gently stopped the door with her hand. "Of course. She's had a rough day." I watched Susan nudge the door open a little more, enough to see inside of the apartment as Steffie backed away.

"So, it's just you and Lucy living here?" Susan asked.

"Just for now." Steffie took a small bite of her toast. "Usually, our mom lives here, too. She's, um, out of town right now, but she should be back very soon."

Susan switched Becky to her other arm, her eyes looking sad. "Honey, I have to ask... how old are you?"

A door slammed somewhere inside.

"Eighteen." Steffie looked irritated, like maybe she'd been asked that question a few other times. "I work at Applebee's. And I'm getting my G.E.D."

Setting Becky down, Susan pulled a small piece of paper and pen from her purse. She wrote something down. "Here's my number. If you need anything—a ride to work, anything—call me, okay?"

Steffie unfolded the paper and studied the money that Susan had tried to sneak into it. "Thanks. That's nice of you, but... me and Lucy... we're good." She handed it back to Susan.

"Okay, well, nice to meet you." When Susan turned, her face was pink, like she was a kid who just got caught doing something bad. She stopped and turned back toward Steffie.

"Please, keep an eye on Lucy. It's been an awful day for these kids."

"Will do, um... Susan." Steffie's face slowly disappeared as the door closed, stopping just long enough to say, "Thanks again for bringing her home."

When we got back to the car, Susan put on some old music and cranked it up but didn't start the engine. After a few minutes of us just sitting there, she turned down the volume. "Steffie and Lucy could really use a break," she said. Her eyes were damp with tears when I saw her face in the rearview mirror. "I wish I could help them. It's just... it's just so frustrating, those kids in that situation." She put her head back and blew out a loud breath. "If I could just get them some money—you know, anonymously."

Nathan's voice was loud as it bounced off the passenger window. "You can."

"What can I do? I" Susan said. "I can't just mail them an envelope filled with cash."

"Not cash. Gift cards."

Susan stared at the windshield for a second. "That's brilliant! We can send them gift cards—for Safeway or Target—in the mail, with no return address. Maybe once a month or something." She reached over and side-hugged Nathan. "My little genius!" His face cracked the tiniest smile.

I know this sounds selfish and maybe even mean, but right then, I didn't really care at all about Lucy. Or her sister—like zero percent. If she hadn't done what she did, maybe my mom might also be helping out Lucy and her sister.

It was late, and finally we were back in our neighborhood. Susan took the usual route to our apartment complex. When we passed by the front of my building, everything looked the same—the same brick walls, the Seattle Seahawks "12" flag covering our neighbor's window on the third floor. It had always felt good to come home to this place. Now, though, after everything that had happened that day, it didn't seem like home at all.

"Theo, do you have a key to your place?" Susan said as she pulled into a parking spot close to me and Mom's apartment.

"Yeah."

"Okay, why don't you run in and get your toothbrush and some clothes. Do you want Nathan to come with you?"

"It's all right." I pushed open the car door. "I'll be right back."

As soon as the key turned in the knob and the door swooshed open, the smell of home hit me. Standing in the dark entryway, it soaked my senses, filling me with the same warmth I'd felt a million times before.

I flipped on the hallway light. At the kitchen table, Rolling Stone magazine was open, showing a story about climate catastrophe and how Florida is in danger of sinking into the ocean in the very near future. Mom's black sweater was draped over the chair. I slid into the seat and rested my head against her sweater. It smelled just like her.

A huge gush of tears burst out of me and I cried really hard for a minute or two. My stomach clenched with each wave of pain. Mom was everywhere, and it was an ache that ate away at my core.

But I didn't want Susan to send Nathan in after me, so I washed my face and gathered up some clothes, my toothbrush and Mom's sweater and stuffed them into my backpack. Grabbing a tissue, I blew my nose and locked the door behind me, struggling to focus on anything but her.

"I was starting to wonder about you," said Susan as I climbed back in next to Becky. "Everything okay?"

"Yep," I said, jamming my backpack between my knees.

That might have been the biggest lie I've ever told.

11

After my dad left, our money situation wasn't great, so my mom worked a lot of extra shifts at the bar. She also tried to be home more, which was pretty much mathematically impossible. Even so, every once in a while she might put on some Chapstick, toss it into her purse and say, "You know what? I think tonight should be an 'I Miss Theo' night."

"Okay!" I'd say, excited that I'd get to hang out with her, even though I wished we could both just stay home. She'd bring me to work and sneak me in through the back, where I'd do my homework sitting on a stool and get free Cokes from Liam, the dishwasher. The last time we'd done this was about a week before the earthquake. Mom had come through the swinging door carrying a tray full of dirty glasses. "Honey, Susan's going to come pick you up in a few. It's a school night."

"Already?" I said.

Stepping out of the dishwasher station, Liam looked at me and said, "Hey, before you bounce, I'll get you a refill." He disappeared into the bar and came back with a fresh Coke. "Your record is six cokes in one night, correct?"

"I lost track," I said, "but I'm not doing that again. Things went kind of bad, you know—stomach-wise." I stuffed my math homework into my backpack and hopped down from the stool.

"Ha, ha!" Liam yanked up the dishwasher lid and shouted through a cloud of steam, "All right, then, take care, my dude."

It would've been fine with me to just stay at Deany's until Mom's shift ended. One or two in the morning was pretty late, but the restaurant was a place where people treated me like I was part of the family. I figured I could easily power through one day of school without falling asleep. But that wasn't my decision to make.

Mom came back in balancing a tall stack of dishes. She set them down and said, "Susan just texted. She's in the parking lot." She slid the dirty plates onto the stainless-steel shelf that Liam stood behind, came up to me and kissed my forehead.

"See you tomorrow, sweetie. Be good for Susan, okay?".

"Always."

She blew me a kiss and backed through the door into the bar.

I remember feeling so warm, so happy that we were making it work without my dad. Things were looking up.

Until they weren't. And as Susan pulled the car into their parking spot, I wedged my knees behind her seat and wrapped my arms around myself to keep my body from shaking.

"You cold?" Becky had her blanket next to her face, brushing her cheek. She stuck the blanket out at me, looked at it, looked at me, and then put it back against her cheek. I didn't want her crusty baby blanket, anyway. When the engine turned off, the silence brought with it a crushing feeling of dread. I was sapped, completely emptied out after an endless day of being yanked from my mom and my home. Nothing seemed like it was mine anymore.

Susan got out of the car and unbuckled Becky, who clung to Susan's neck like a baby monkey dragging her feet across the seat on the way out. It was my turn to get out, but I was so exhausted I couldn't force my muscles to move. Then, as I climbed out of the car and the cool air hit my face, I realized what might help erase the terrible, helpless feeling.

I needed to do something. Even if it seemed crazy, I had to try to find my mom. And as far as I could tell, the only real way to ease this overwhelming helpless feeling was to make my way back to the waterfront. In fact, I really wanted to just take off running right then, but I knew it had to be planned out a lot better than that to even have a chance.

I went with Susan, Becky and Nathan up the outside stairs, checking out the area around outside the apartment complex. If I could make it to this stairway, I'd be able to get away in no time. As tired as I felt, it energized me to feel a plan forming. I would hang out for a while, making sure to be as cool and calm as possible so that Susan might stop worrying about me. I'd wait until people started doing other stuff, or until they went to bed, and I'd slip out. Couldn't be that hard, I figured, especially since everyone had to be as exhausted as I was.

A swell of energy filled me. This idea could work. My mind was bouncing around a million different places as we reached the top floor. *I wonder if Nathan has a bike. Probably not; I'd never seen him ride one. I could take the bus. I have the ten bucks Mom gave me for souvenirs. I can't use a ten-dollar bill on the Metro, walk to 7-11 and get change Perfect.*

Susan held Becky in one arm and opened the door. She kicked a pink ball out of the way and turned on the kitchen light. "Fries, Mommy! Want fries."

She plopped Becky in her highchair. "Okay, sweetheart. Nathan, do me a favor and get some plates and napkins."

It happened so fast. The smell of stale fries started the whole thing, making my gut lurch, and once the door closed, I felt smothered. The room got instantly hot and stuffy, like it was low on oxygen. Everything smelled terrible. I brushed the back of my hand along my forehead and felt a slimy layer of sweat. I leaned against the counter as the room tilted, squinting at Nathan to keep him in focus. My legs started buzzing with pins and needles like they were going to sleep. As I watched Nathan reach for napkins, a gray fog closed in on him and everything else. The pins and needles filled up my body, then head, and then everything went black.

12

"Theo? Theo, wake up!"

I opened my eyes. I was laying down. My head throbbed and my mouth felt sticky and dry. The ceiling light shining down from behind their heads made Nathan and Susan look like dark, hovering creatures.

"You fainted," said Nathan.

"That was a little scary," Susan said. "We barely caught you. You almost hit your head on the counter." She pressed a cold washcloth over my forehead and dabbed my cheeks. "Nathan, get Theo some water, please. You're looking better, hon. Got some color back, thank goodness. You were looking pretty green there."

As I came out of the fog, a zillion images flooded my head: Sylvia's bloody nose—Mom floating out of sight—and, *that's right, I have a plan.*

"Do you feel like eating something?" Susan asked, lifting up the back of my head and sliding the cool washcloth under my neck.

"Um, sure." I tried to prop myself up.

"Easy there," Susan said. "Take your time." She held out her hand.

"You're probably running on fumes, which is why you passed out. Grab onto my hands, honey." She gently pulled me to my feet. I still felt a little woozy, but definitely better than right before everything went black.

Becky didn't seem too concerned at all, sitting on the carpet talking to her board books, but Nathan wouldn't take his eyes off me. At the kitchen table, Susan pushed some papers aside, pulled out a chair and set down a plate holding my burger and fries. "Theo, do you want these microwaved?"

"No thanks." Microwaved fries sounded worse to me than cold ones. As I'd expected, they were limp and warm-ish, but you'd still think that after going all day without food, a bacon cheeseburger would taste pretty good. Not the case. It didn't taste like anything. My brain was too messed up at the moment to appreciate the taste of food, but I still wolfed everything down with the help of lots of ketchup packets. As I ate, I couldn't stop wondering what was going on down at the waterfront. There must have been more information by now, more news—*that's it, the news.*

"Susan, can you put on the news?"

Placing a pink sippy cup on Becky's highchair tray, she gave me the same sad puppy look as when she first saw me in the hospital. "You've got a lot to process, honey." She leaned down and wrapped a Dora the Explorer bib around Becky. "And remember what Sergeant Loden said? She'll let us know as soon as they learn anything. I think it would be best if we all just had some quiet time."

Ugh. I was so tired of being treated like a little kid. I'd seen dead bodies earlier that day. Had Susan?

"Susan, please?" I said, "you already said I can't go back there. Can we at least see what's going on?" *Swallow, breathe,* I told myself. I wouldn't be convincing her of anything by whining like a baby. Watching Susan shift her glance between the TV and me, I could tell she was thinking about it.

"I'll tell you what," she said, "we'll watch it for half an hour, but then no more for the rest of the night. Deal?"

"Yes, deal!" I said. "Thanks."

Nathan shoveled some Frosty into his mouth with a straw and reached for the remote. "Probably on CNN," he said. "Channel 206." Instantly, the red CNN logo appeared at the bottom corner of the screen. The video was of Elliott Bay from up in the sky, earlier in the day when it was still light out. A wide, jagged line of brown sludge with chunks of white and black snaked all down the shoreline. Susan gasped, then muffled it with the palm of her hand.

"The tsunami was caused by a magnitude 5.6 earthquake," said the reporter's voice. "Officials have confirmed that most of the destruction occurred along the Seattle waterfront and Alki Beach. Despite the damage you see, the tremor was considerably smaller than the quake that hit the Seattle Fault eleven hundred years ago—"

"That one was a 9.2," said Nathan.

The reporter went on, "And caused far less damage to the infrastructure than had been modeled by the State of Washington for a quake this size. While significant incidents of power outage and bridge damage have been reported, essential services still appear to be functioning throughout the Puget Sound area."

My heart pounded as I searched for any speck that might be Mom, but obviously the camera was way too high to make out any actual people. The four of us sat there, lit up in the dark living room by the glow of the screen. I had to stretch my neck to see past Becky, who had decided that right in front of the TV was a good place to set up her Barbie house.

"Becky, honey, move please." Susan sprang off the couch, scooped up Becky and her toys and placed them to the side.

"Forgive me," said the voice of another announcer, "but I need to break in here. We're now going live to Harborview Medical Center for a press briefing about casualties. Let's take a listen."

The overhead view disappeared and cut to two women in clean, white doctor coats standing at a microphone. Behind them were the doors to the emergency room.

"As you can imagine," said the taller doctor, "an event like this creates major challenges due to the large variety of incidents and locations where they occur. And I'd like to take this opportunity to commend the dedicated first responders and emergency professionals who have been instrumental in saving so many lives today."

A voice from the crowd: "Can you comment on casualties?"

"As of now," said the shorter woman, "107 victims of the tsunami have been admitted to the hospital. Out of that number, 63 are in satisfactory condition, 27 are serious or critical... and 17 were deceased upon arrival."

"That means dead," said Nathan.

My mouth instantly dried out, but I forced the tears to stay behind my eyeballs. This was no time to lose it again.

"Okay, bad idea by me," said Susan, grabbing the remote from Nathan's hand. "I think we've seen more than enou..."

"No, Susan." My voice was shaky. "You promised. A half hour!"

"He's right," Nathan said, "it's only been seven minutes."

"We need to cut away again," said the announcer. "It appears we have some breaking news right now. Let's go live to Parv Sommerstein. Parv?"

"Thanks, Wes. I'm here with Otto James, who managed to make it out of the tsunami zone along with his wife, Sylvia."

"It's Otto!" I yelled. "Susan, you can't turn it off! It's the old man we were with when it happened!"

Otto stood in front of a Harborview Medical Center sign, smiling the same crooked smile that he'd been doing when he heard the sirens. In his hands were a couple of paper coffee cups with black lids. That was a good sign, I figured. Sylvia must be doing okay, enough to drink coffee, at least.

"Mr. James, if you don't mind, please describe your ordeal earlier today," said the reporter, pushing the microphone closer to Otto's face.

"I really only have one thing to say." Otto looked straight at the camera. Some brave young folks helped my wife Sylvia and me today." His mouth quivered. "And furthermore, I'm fully convinced that if it weren't for them, neither she nor I would have surv—" His voice cracked and he got quiet for a few seconds.

The reporter reached out and patted his shoulder. "I know this is difficult, sir. Please, take your time."

Otto blew a loud breath into the microphone and went on. "One fellow was particularly courageous. I haven't seen him since we were pulled out of harm's way, and I just... well, I just want to thank him."

"Mr. James," said the reporter, "can you tell us this hero's name?"

Otto tilted his head, leaned into the camera and said, "His name is Theo—"

It was like he was only looking at me.

"Theo Cloverdale."

13

Otto went on to describe everything, from meeting Nathan and me on the bridge to getting knocked around in the earthquake. And from Nathan pulling Lucy in to how we all had to hang on to the foam board. And finally, how I helped Sylvia to keep Otto from drowning.

"Theo," Otto said, "I just hope you're out there somewhere, watching this. Sylvia and I—" His voice started to crack. "We, um—well—we owe you our—our lives." He pulled out a tissue and dabbed his eyes, awkwardly scraping his glasses against his nose.

I leaned back and stared at the ceiling, wondering if that had really just happened.

"I knew we shouldn't be watching this." Susan sprung from the couch, grabbed the remote from Nathan and punched the TV off. "He shouldn't have said your name like that."

"That was seen all over the world," said Nathan.

"Thanks for pointing that out," I said.

Becky waddled over and stuck an orange book in Susan's face. "Green

Ham, Mommy. Read Green Ham."

"Sit on Mommy's lap, sweetie."

Becky tried to climb up, but she couldn't do it with the book under her arm. Finally, Susan lifted her up.

"Guys," she said, "Becky's right. We need to step away from all of this for a while. We all could use a little break, wouldn't you say?"

"Yeah," I said, "but the news tells us stuff as it actually happens. It's the best way to get information—"

"I'd like you guys to do something else, okay?" Susan was serious, and she was looking at me. "Instead of watching a bunch of reporters milk this story, how about if we trust Sergeant Loden to tell us when she has some real information."

Fine, I thought. The sooner we wrapped the night up, the sooner I could get out of there.

"I got some new Pokémon cards," said Nathan. "Want to see them?"

"Uh, sure," I said. It might've seemed obvious that that was the last thing I wanted to do, but he sure didn't seem to notice as I followed him into his room. Like his desk at school, Nathan's room was super neat and orderly. It was completely the opposite of the rest of the apartment—his bed was made, his floor was totally clear of clothes and toys. On the desk sat a chess set, ready for someone to make the first move. While Nathan pulled out his notebooks, I sat on the floor and leaned against his bed. A *Fantastic Structures of the World* poster covered up most of his closet door. It had been up there as long as I could remember—Hoover Dam, the Great Wall of China, the Golden Gate Bridge—I'd already read everything on that poster at some time or another. Now I just stared at it as millions of random thoughts pulsed through my head.

Nathan gently set the folder down, opened the cover and pried back a clear plastic sleeve. "These are my new ones. I can do a Bolt Beam with this one." He removed the cards and lined them up on the floor. "This one is UU, but these two can be Sweepers or Hazers. Here's an Aerial Ace."

Pokémon's fun to play sometimes, like when you don't have anything else to do, but at that moment, watching Nathan go through each card had to be one of the most boring things a person could do other than staring at a rock. Mom always said that patience was something she admired most in people, but this was asking for more a lot more patience than I currently had. I tried to focus on the cards, but before long my butt started hurting, then my leg fell asleep and I was feeling done. Lucky for me, that's when Susan came in.

"Guys, it's late. You both must be worn out. Theo, I set up a place on the couch for you."

"Okay, thanks," I said. *And sweet,* I thought. Sleeping on the couch would make it a lot easier to get out than if I had to sleep on the floor in Nathan's room. I stood up and felt the prickly tingles of my leg waking up. While Nathan carefully put away his Pokémons, I backed my way toward the door.

"All right, well, see you tomorrow," I said.

He pushed himself onto the bed without looking at me and lifted the Pokémon notebook onto his lap. "Night."

I almost tripped over Becky on the way out, since she was sitting in the middle of the hallway, chewing on her blanket and flipping through another book with her slimy baby fingers.

"Sorry, Theo," Susan said, scooping her up. "Come on, Becky Bug. One more story, then it's time to go night-night." She kissed the top of Becky's head and sniffed her wet hair. "Mmm, you smell so nice after a bath. Theo, let me know if you need anything."

"Okay."

"And honey... it's going to be okay." She put her arm around me. "You know that, right?"

"Yep," I lied.

"Try to get some sleep, okay? Trust me, things always seem better in the morning." The door to Susan's bedroom closed and I turned for the living room.

Finally, I was alone. I dropped onto the couch and kicked off my shoes. The second my head hit the pillow, everything started again. Images played in my brain from the day: my mom in the tree, her looking at me as she fell in the water, then floating further and further, then disappearing behind the Spaghetti Factory. So many images of water—water rising, churning, covering everything and then going back out. And the body. And the other body. *Stop!* a voice deep inside me shrieked.

I rolled onto my side and started thinking about my class. I went over the kids that I'd seen down the hill by Mr. Sharrard when the wave hit. Their faces stacked up in my mind.

Jennifer Cartwright—nice person. I had a crush on her in third grade and Kenny found out and told her. She was cool about it and we're just friends now. She was taking a selfie by the eraser sculpture when the first wave hit.

Calvin Jasper—He could draw anime better than anyone I knew. He was trapped, standing on a bench, surrounded by water and crying.

Jhari Ren—he could do a great Cartman imitation because his parents let him watch South Park. He was trying to make it up the hill but kept sliding backwards.

So many other people, like Maria, who lived in our apartment building, and Hector Alvarez, who found my tooth on the playground in fourth grade. That was pretty funny. The whole soccer game stopped, and everybody started looking for it like a treasure hunt or something. I saw him fall into the water while trying to make it up the fake tree.

They must've been found by now, I tried to convince myself. *It's not like they were out in the middle of the ocean or something.* Actually, I knew better; Puget Sound was as freezing cold as the Pacific Ocean. Earlier in the year we did a science unit on the local waterways, learning about the sea life—starfish, octopuses, sea anemones—and how chilly the water is where they live.

"In forty-six-degree water," Mr. Sharrard had said, "without a cold-water survival suit, you'd be in big trouble. After about forty-five minutes, you're exhausted. And if you're in there for over an hour or two, you're a goner."

Lying down wasn't working. All it did was make the movie start back up in my head and my body couldn't get comfortable. I sat up and threw off my blanket, then stood up and stumbled my way down the hall and into the bathroom. Cranking the water to full-on cold, I figured a nice splash of icy water might distract me, even if it was for just a second. I dried my face and noticed a bottle of hand sanitizer on the counter like the one Mr. Sharrard kept on his desk.

I remembered how he was always on the class about having clean hands. Bottles of sanitizer were placed all over the classroom, because he was basically right—we were kind of a gritty group. Kenny puked in his lunch box last fall and in the sink just after we'd come back from mid-winter break. Noah Frazier was a daily snot snorter, which grossed out pretty much everybody. Mr. Sharrard didn't make a big deal out of it, but he would review proper hygiene with us every few weeks. To be honest, it was fine with me when he called us out sometimes.

"Welcome back, Room 302," he'd said one day as we all came in from recess. "Smells like you got some exercise. Well, good on you. Please don't forget to stop at one of our convenient sanitizing stations positioned throughout the room or help yourself to the more luxurious choice of soap and water." He pumped a squirt of sanitizer into his palm. "We want to have clean thespians for our next project."

Nathan was already sitting in his seat with his hands folded on the desktop.

"What's a thespian?" I sat down and asked him.

"An actor."

Mr. Sharrard liked to do fun stuff with the class, if we earned it, that is. He walked over to his closet and pulled out his director's chair, the one he used to read us stories. He unfolded it front and center and sat down. "Now who's ready to participate in the dramatic arts?"

Nathan raised his hand.

"Hmm, a single volunteer. Impressive, people." Standing up and grabbing a stack of papers from his desk, Mr. Sharrard said, "As you know, your assignment was to read the script of a famous radio play. Raise your hand if you've done the assignment."

Up went Nathan's hand again, plus mine and a few other kids'.

"Okay, then, it looks like those who raised their hands are entitled to be members of our cast. The rest of you can be our studio audience. Think about showing up prepared next time." He loudly cleared his throat and cranked up his teacher voice. "Today, we'll be performing *The Invisible Man,* an audio play based on the 1897 novella by H.G. Wells. For those of you who aren't yet familiar, it's the story of Griffin, an English scientist." Mr. Sharrard reached for his coffee cup and took a sip. "Through his research, Griffin develops a way to make himself invisible. Who here might appreciate the opportunity to disappear every once in a while?"

"Right here," said Lucy, throwing her arm in the air.

"Well, there's just one catch," Mr. Sharrard said in a much quieter voice. "Once he discovers how to make himself invisible, he's unable to come up with a way to become visible again—and he slowly—slowly, goes— insane!"

My butt jumped in my seat, and I could hear random little screams and yelps.

"Nathan," Mr. Sharrard said, "since at the moment, you appear the most enthusiastic among your fellow scholars, I'll give you first choice of the acting roles. Who's it going to be?"

Nathan looked down at his desk. "I'll be Griffin, the Invisible Man."

"Excellent choice," Mr. Sharrard said. "Life's good when you're top of the bill. Just ask our man, Dwayne 'The Rock' Johnson." A single eyebrow arched up above his eye as he looked at Nathan. "But are you sure you don't mind playing the part of a deranged, murderous lunatic?"

Nathan's face was blank. "Yes."

The class laughed while Mr. Sharrard opened a gym bag and started pulling out random things: cups and bottles, a coconut shell, different-sized bells. "You're probably wondering what all this stuff is for. These are called props. Stuff like this was used to create sound effects for radio shows. Yes, Kenny?"

"What's a radio show?"

"Excellent question! One that deserves a clang of cowbell." He picked up the heavy metal bell and whacked it hard with a drumstick.

"Back in the mid-20th Century, years before there was YouTube or even TV, people would gather around their radios and listen to shows—drama, comedy, suspense—and take part in what was then referred to as 'theater of the mind'."

"No video?" Lucy said.

"No video," said Mr. Sharrard. Picking out two small bowls and tapping them lightly on Lucy's desk, he talked above the "clip-clop clip-clop" sound they were making. "Sounds like a horse trotting, yes?"

I had to admit, this sounded pretty fun.

"So, here's what we're going to do." Mr. Sharrard placed the cowbell and a drumstick on Kenny's desk. Kenny tapped the bell softly, making a light *clink* sound. "I'll edit our performance on my home computer and we'll listen to our finished masterpiece during lunch on Friday. Sound good?"

No one answered.

Mr. Sharrard groaned. "Lovin' the enthusiasm, folks. Okay, well then, since you all appear to have stage fright, I'll assign the parts." He looked down at his iPad. "Conner, you're going to be Thomas Marvel. Theo, you'll be Dr. Kemp. Okay, let's see, Caryn, we'll put you down as Janny Hall—"

I felt a tap on my shoulder.

"Seems like when Mr. Sharrard asks for volunteers, everyone is the invisible man," said Nathan.

I sniffed. "Good one."

****

Now, as I lounged on Susan's couch like a useless piece of meat, I wondered if anything would ever be funny again. I couldn't stop feeling like something bad, something really bad, was just waiting for the right time to smack me down even further. I thought about Mom—again. And the water, throwing her all over the place and sucking her out of sight. And Sylvia's face—covered in blood. And Lucy—me and Nathan pulling her out just in time.

And I had recorded it. That was the other thing—I had literally stood there taking video as the wave hit. I reached down to the floor for my phone and thought about what was on it now. *Is it going to freak me out? Probably, in fact, definitely.* But if it did, I reminded myself to freak out silently or risk Susan coming back out. I unplugged my phone from the charger and looked at some of the photos from earlier in the day. When I realized they were making me cry, I decided watching any videos would have to wait. No use torturing myself.

After what felt like forever, I waited another fifteen minutes just to make sure everyone was asleep. It was tense and boring at the same time. The clock moved painfully slow, like when you're staring at a plate of cheesy tater tots and you're so excited that you're almost drooling, but the ketchup just won't leave the bottle.

I couldn't stay still for another second. Tiptoeing to the door, I picked up my shoes. They were still damp. Backpack? Where was my backpack? I took a deep breath. No problem, it was wedged under the coffee table. Then I heard something. There was a low hum coming from down the hall. I took another long gulp of air and held my breath. It was someone snoring, probably Nathan. Moving gently toward the door, my foot brushed against something. I looked down and realized I'd come within an inch of kicking Becky's plastic cow car across the room and waking up the whole place.

I took a couple more deep breaths to calm down, then shuffled silently toward the door. I turned the knob, but it wouldn't give. *Dead bolt.* I turned the latch, and it made a short, *clok clok* sound. At that point, I knew there was no turning back. The door opened, giving off the stale odor of the hall-way. My heart felt like it was about to explode, and that Susan or Nathan or maybe even Becky would find me in the morning, dead on their welcome mat. Easing the door shut behind me, I walked away from the apartment. I felt stronger and faster with each step. When I hit the parking lot, I started into a slow jog. *Perfect,* I thought, *I can be down at the water in less than an hour if the bus—*

"Theo?"

I jerked to a stop. *I know that voice.* I turned around and my eyes found him, outlined against the blue light of the parking lot, chirping his car locked. He had a puzzled look on his face as he walked toward me.

"What are you doing out here?" he said.

Wow, I thought. *Of all the times, he chooses now to show up.* I blew out a foggy breath and shoved my hands in my pockets.

"Hey, Dad."

14

"I got here as soon as I could," he said. Without any warning, he sprung toward me and smothered me in a hug. I could taste his cologne in my nose as my cheek brushed against his slick green tracksuit. He backed away and looked me up and down. Little tangles of hair sprung out of his man bun and there were streaks of gray in his beard. He definitely looked different than he had the last time I'd seen him.

"Seriously, what are you doing out here, buddy?" he said. "It's late. Is everything okay?"

"Yep, I'm good," I said. Of course, I was the opposite of good, but he didn't need to know about it. His smell was trapped in my sinuses, and I wanted to blow my nose.

"You look like you're headed somewhere in a hurry," he said.

"I—I don't know."

"What do you mean you don't know?" He pulled back the sleeve of his jacket and checked his big, silver wristwatch. "It's after ten, for goodness sakes. Where the heck are you going?"

I was too tired to think up a lie, even a bad one, so I just spilled it. "I'm going to look for Mom."

"You're what?"

"I'm going back to the water to look for—"

"No, no, I heard you. But you can't just go by yourself. You're only nine—"

"I'm eleven."

"Sorry, eleven. How were you going to get down there?"

I backed away a couple more steps and looked down the street. If I took off running, he'd have to catch me while wearing Crocs, and who knows, one could fly off and I'd have a better chance of getting away. "Bus."

"Wait, seriously, you were just going to hop on a bus and—"

"Whatever."

"Theo, I can't let you do that. You know it's not safe."

A rush of rage washed over me. "Since when did you care?" I said. "You can't stop me."

"Oh, yes I can—all right, look—" His voice got softer, but his eyes were still just hollow shadows in the dim light of the parking lot. "We'll find her together, okay? Just you and me."

I backed away, adding more space between us. "Like I said, I'm good." I turned and started jogging, out of the parking lot and onto the sidewalk. Even though it was a relief to be away from him, it didn't take long for the truth to sink in. My dad would obviously catch me before I could get bus money, let alone find a bus to get on. I could hear him yelling my name in the distance, his Crocs thwapping against the sidewalk.

"Theo, hold up!"

I made it a couple of blocks, all the way to the gas pumps in front of the 7-11 when I finally felt his grip on my shoulder. The squeeze got harder, and I came to a sudden stop.

"Ow! Don't touch me!" I yelled.

He let go and slouched over, his hands resting on his knees. "I'll... go...

with you," he wheezed, pulling out the rubber band and redoing his hair.

A guy walked out of the store. He looked at me, then at my dad, all bent over and out of breath. "Evening," he said, smacking a pack of cigarettes against his hand and disappearing into the night.

My dad slowly straightened himself up and ran the back of his hand across his mouth. "We'll look for her together." He spat a glob of stringy spit onto the pavement. "I've been frantically trying to get a hold of you. Cell service has been really spotty."

"Why do you all of a sudden care about me? Or Mom? You never did before."

"I told you, Theo, that's just not true. I've always cared about you and your mother. I just—"

The screech of tires jolted both of us. The red car squealed to a stop, crossways between two gas pumps. Its driver's door flew open...and Susan popped out.

"Oh, Theo, thank goodness I found you!" Susan stood there, holding her phone out and pointing at it. Her cheeks were streaked with tears. "Julie, your social worker, just called. I went to tell you and you were gone and—"

"What'd she say?" I said.

"They found your mom..."

"Is she..." I couldn't finish the question. Every muscle in my body knotted into little, tight balls. *Here it comes*, I thought. *They found her. They found her but it's too late.* I tried to prepare myself for the worst news I would ever hear.

Susan's voice echoed in the parking lot.

"She's alive!"

15

It took a second for me to realize I wasn't standing up. In fact, I was on my butt. "They found her?" I mumbled. I wish I could describe how this felt, but everything went numb. The only thing I could feel was a river of tears pouring down my cheeks.

My dad came over and put his hands on my shoulders, half patting me, half shaking me. "Can you believe it?" His grin was huge, his teeth looking frosty blue in the gas station lights. "They found her!"

I picked myself up off the pavement and ducked away from him, leaving his arms hugging the air. "How is she?" I shouted. "Where is she?"

Susan sniffed. "I'm so sorry, honey, but the only info I got is that she's alive and at Harborview Hospital and—" She dabbed at her eyes with a tissue and glared at my dad. "Hello, Mitch." She looked at him like she'd just eaten a slug, but her face quickly turned back to nice as she shifted her attention to me. "Go with your dad, Theo. I'll meet you at the hospital as soon as I can get my mom over to watch the kids. Well, what are you waiting for?" she said. "Go!"

I took off running back toward the apartment parking lot. My feet felt like they'd barely touched the ground and I left my dad in the dust. I was waiting for him when he finally got there and unlocked the doors to his car. As I got in, I thought again about what Susan had said. *Should I be happy Mom's alive? Of course, I thought, but alive can mean awake and talking or it can mean almost dead or anything in between.*

"Put on your seatbelt," my dad said.

As I clicked it into place, a tornado of what-ifs swirled through my head. Mom could be bruised and scraped up, but okay. Or she could be lying there asleep with millions of tubes sticking out. The possibilities were choking my brain. I forced myself to focus on the dashboard in front of me, on all of the digital displays and colors and information that came with my dad's fancy car. The inside of it was perfect in every way, not even a single candy wrapper on the floor or crumb in a seat crack.

"Sorry it took me so long to get to you," Dad said. His face glowed orange as he stared ahead. "The cell phone towers must've been overloaded or something."

We pulled onto 35th Avenue, not talking at all until we hit the West Seattle Bridge. "So, um, how have you been?" he asked. "I mean... you know, besides what happened today?"

What do you mean, "besides what happened today?" I wanted to scream at him. "What happened today" had made it the worst day of my life. Instead, I just said, "Fine."

The inside of the car was filled with the smell of his cologne. It was disgusting and I'd forgotten that about him, that he'd always been into that stuff. It was so thick I could taste it. What made things even more annoying was that the traffic was super slow. Once every two or three minutes, we'd move another few feet. Emergency vehicles were everywhere—police cars on the side of the road, utility trucks and fire engines scattered among the Hondas and Priuses—and nobody was making much progress.

My dad switched on some sort of motivational business Podcast, so we didn't talk again until we were almost at the hospital. "So, I have to ask," he said, as we finally exited I-5 and started up the hill toward Harborview. "How did you escape the tsunami when, you know, all those other people didn't?"

Of every person on the planet, my dad was probably the one who I least wanted to discuss the tsunami with. "I don't know," I said. "Me and some other people were higher up the hill."

"And that's all there is to it?"

I shrugged. "Pretty much."

"Wow." He reached over and squeezed my shoulder. "My son, the escape artist." The tires squealed as we turned up the ramp of the parking garage.

Nothing like learning from the best, I thought.

Julie was in the lobby of the hospital's trauma unit when we walked in.

"Hi, Theo. Is this your dad?"

"Where is she?" I said, walking past her.

"Whoa, hang on," said my dad, but I didn't pay any attention. I wasn't about to wait another second, and if I had to check every room to find her, that's what I was going to do.

Julie's voice jolted me. "Theo!"

I stopped. It reminded me of Mom's serious voice. "Just hang on one second," she said. "We need to talk first, then I'll take you to your mom."

It was a gut punch to be that close. "I'm Julie Nevers," she said, holding out her hand to my dad. "I was assigned to help Theo when you couldn't be located."

"I really appreciate that." He smiled and shook her hand. "Mitch Cloverdale."

"Let's all have a seat real quick," she said.

Seriously? I thought. *Is she torturing me on purpose?* We followed her down the hall, into a little room with puffy chairs and a TV that was playing footage of the tsunami aftermath. A couple of reporters' faces were framed in the top corner of the screen. Julie grabbed the remote and powered off the TV as me and my dad took seats on the stained, lumpy couch.

She sat on the arm of a chair across from us. "Earlier tonight, your mom was spotted by a Coast Guard helicopter." She paused, stared at the ceiling and went on. "This is going to sound really crazy, so take a deep breath."

Starting with when Mom was first found, Julie told us every detail of how she had been rescued.

"Wow!" said my dad. His head dropped into his hands. "That's—that's amazing. Unbelievable. I mean—just, wow."

"What's amazing," said Julie, "is that she was able to survive for so long under those circumstances. She's tough... and pretty lucky."

"Can I just see her please?" I was trying so hard to not make my voice any whinier, but I felt like I was going to burst into flames if I had to sit there any longer.

"Yes, of course," Julie said, standing up. "I just wanted you to know. She's asleep right now... and she's on a ventilator."

"A what?" The constant throat lump was something I'd gotten used to, but this one had inflated to the size of a tennis ball.

"It's a tube that helps her breathe," Julie said. "You might see some other equipment too, but trust me, it looks a lot scarier than it actually is."

"Okay, that's it then?" I stood up and started walking down the hallway.

"Theo," Julie said, jogging up to me and turning me around. "It's this way. I'll show you." We took the elevator up a couple of floors, turned right, and next to the double doors was a sign that said *Intensive Care Unit*. The door buzzed open, and we walked around to the other side of the nurses' station. "Right there," Julie pointed. "Room 317."

As I was about to go in, the door opened. Standing there was Dr. Kumasaka. "Hello," she said in a quiet voice. "She's asleep. Probably will be for a while."

The whole way over, I'd imagined how it would feel when I saw Mom. *Will it be painful? A relief? Will she even look like I Mom?* As crazy as it sounds, right then I really couldn't remember what she looked like.

Dr. Kumasaka moved out of the doorway, giving me a clear view. When I saw Mom lying so still, I stopped thinking completely. Her right arm was wrapped in bandages and rested in a straight line down the side of her body. And that thing that Julie had mentioned—the ventilator—was creepy. It fed oxygen through a long tube that went into her mouth, down her throat and into her airway. This machine did Mom's breathing for her, making her upper body rise and fall with each breath. *Whoosh… whoosh.*

I eased myself onto the edge of her bed. A gallon of tears filled my eyes and poured down my face. I struggled to form the only word I could think to say.

"Mom," I whispered, burying my head in the side of her pillow. She still smelled like my mom, even through all the other hospital smells in the room. My body shook a little, but I was careful not to mess with any of the tubes that surrounded her body. I closed my eyes, never so sad and happy at the same time.

"When your mom arrived, her body temperature was very low," said Dr. Kumasaka. "We had to warm her to get it back up, then it got too high, so we did some tests and found out she's got a lung infection."

I sat up, sniffed and looked at the doctor. "How bad is it?"

She pulled off her glasses. "Well, rest is the best way for our bodies to fight infections. We've put her into what's called an induced coma."

"She's in a coma?" I said.

"It's more like a deep sleep," said the doctor. "It's something we can control."

I stood up and Dr. Kumasaka handed me a tissue.

"Is she going to be okay?" I was careful to say it quietly as if I might accidentally wake Mom up.

"We have every reason to believe that your mom will be just fine, Theo. And we're doing everything we can to make sure of it." Dr. Kumasaka crossed her arms. "But infections can be tricky, so the important thing is that we stay positive and—"

"That's it? After all this?" The words shot out of me before I even realized it. I pointed at Mom, at all the machines stacked around her, all the beeping and buzzing and whooshing. "Staying positive is going to bring her temperature down?" I yelled. "Is it going to cure her infection?" A fresh storm of tears and snot poured down my face. "She's got to be okay! She has to!"

"Theo." I could feel my dad's hand on my shoulder. "She's—"

"Leave me alone!" I took his hand and flung it like a Frisbee. "You don't even know her! You left her!"

Dr. Kumasaka led my dad to a chair by the sink. She came back and crouched down in front of my face. "Theo," she said, "Look, I don't want you to be discouraged. But you seem like the kind of guy who appreciates knowing the truth, even if it's a little rough."

"I guess," I sniffed.

"Okay, then, yes, your mom is pretty sick. The good news is, her organs are working well. Her blood pressure is stabilized and frankly, her color is a lot better than it was when she arrived. She needs us to be strong right now, okay? Just like she is."

I could hear the door opening behind me. "Oh, oh, my gosh!" Susan's hand covered her mouth, and her face was bright pink. Behind her, Nathan stood still in the doorway. Tears were pouring down Susan's cheeks as she moved next to my mom. She leaned over and rested her head on Mom's good shoulder. "Hi, honey," she whispered. "You're gonna be okay, sweetie. Just rest." Susan brushed Mom's hair out of her face and lightly kissed her forehead. "We love you."

Sniffing sounds came from behind me, around where Julie was standing. The only other noise in the room was Mom's ventilator. *Whoosh, whoosh.* Nathan's voice broke the silence. "Continuous mandatory ventilation relies on patient-initiated breaths. It's often used for short-term therapy and in critical care environments."

"That's correct. Impressive," said Dr. Kumasaka. "Theo, you can stay for a while, but she needs to get some rest."

"Take your time, son," said my dad. "When you're ready to go, we'll go to your mom's place and pick up your stuff.

"You'll be staying with me."

16

I was in third grade when my dad moved out. I'll always remember the night he left. It was late and I was in bed. It was Mom's voice that woke me up.

"You said it was over, Mitch."

"It is over."

I had gotten up, shuffled over to the door and stuck my ear against it.

"You're lying!" Mom growled. "Did you really think I'd forgotten what her perfume smells like?" Mom's voice got softer. "It makes me sick to my stomach. Take your stinking flowers and get out!" Something smashed against the wall.

"Katie, whoa, hang on. Just listen to me for a sec—"

"Mitch, I am done listening to you—I'm done trusting you." Her loud whisper was easier to hear than a yell.

I heard footsteps and voices getting further away so I opened my door a crack.

"I want you out of here," said Mom.

"What about Theo? He's my son, too!"

"We will discuss that later." Her voice got quieter, but not by much. "Tomorrow night, I'm taking him out for a movie or something. When we get back, you need to be gone."

There was a long silence, then my dad's voice. "Really?" His stupid chuckle made me so mad I wanted to punch him. "Where am I supposed to go?"

"That's your problem," said Mom. "I can think of one fairly obvious option."

A door slammed and the voices stopped.

And that was it. By the time me and Mom had gotten back from the movie at Southcenter the next night, Dad and all his stuff were gone. No phone calls. No texts. Just gone. After that, I guess he didn't care that I missed him, because he definitely didn't seem to miss me.

Susan's question to my dad brought me back to the hospital room. "Mitch, can we chat out in the hallway for a second?"

"Uh, sure." My dad stepped around Julie, and Susan followed him out.

After hearing my parents argue so much, I'd gotten pretty good at understanding soft voices, the kind where you can hear the *t*'s and *p*'s and *sh*'s, then figure it out from there. Listening to Dad and Julie whispering in the hallway outside Mom's room wasn't much different.

"Mitch," Susan said, "Katie and I have an arrangement. We watch each other's kids. Our boys are good for each other. And frankly, when was the last time you saw Theo? Two years ago? Maybe three?"

Dad blew out a loud breath and whispered, "Susan, the bottom line is, I'm his father. And if Katie can't take care of him—"

"I think it's a mistake, Mitch," said Susan. "At least let him deal with his trauma in a place where he feels comfortable, a place he knows."

No one talked for a few seconds, then my dad said, "I appreciate your concern, Susan, and I understand your point." His voice became softer, but sharp. "But I'm his father. He's coming with me—tonight."

I'd never even been to my dad's house. Where would I sleep? And did that mean I had to live with his girlfriend Amber, too? The thought of it made me cringe. I could hear the sounds of Susan's and my dad's footsteps coming back in. Dad entered the room first, wearing a fake smile on his face.

A buzzing sound went off and Dr. Kumasaka looked at her phone. "Okay," she said. "It's time for Katie to get some rest. I promise we'll let you know if anything changes."

I walked over to Nathan, who was staring out the window at the city lights. "I guess I'm going with him," I said, nodding toward my dad.

"Okay."

"All right, well, I guess I'll see you at schoo—" *Wait. School?* I thought. *What will school be like?* The idea rocked me. *Who will be our teacher? Which kids will be there? And who won't?* "I guess I'll see you around," I said.

"Ready, son?" My dad jingled the keys in his pocket.

I leaned down and put my head next to Mom's. *Please wake up!* I screamed inside my brain. *Right now! I don't want to go with him! Can't you hear me? I don't want to go with him!* But her eyes didn't open, her feet didn't even move a tiny bit under the sheets.

"Bye, Mom. I love you," whispered. I kissed her head, stood up and the four of us walked in silence to the elevators. Susan looked super mad, like she really wanted to yell at my dad, but she just stared straight ahead. Her face was sour and her lips were pressed together so hard they were white. The elevator door opened, and we rode silently to Level B, where our cars were parked next to each other.

"I have something for you," Nathan said. He opened the passenger door, reached inside and pulled out a plastic bag.

"What is it?" I said.

He handed it to me and I looked inside—there were two packs of Pokémon cards. "Cool," I said, reaching in and checking out one of them. "Thanks."

"You're welcome. It's a Neo Genesis Hotfoot Deck."

Susan came over and gave me a hug. "I'll call you tomorrow. Text or call, anytime, okay?"

"Okay." I walked to my dad's car and slid into the passenger seat. Before I could even buckle my seatbelt, his fancy Mercedes was backing out.

Closing my eyes, I let it sink in. *She's alive.* Mom was alive and they were taking care of her, and everything was going to be all right. I leaned back in the softness of the seat and blew out a long, cleansing breath. It was like a warm blanket had been draped over me. It made me realize how tight my muscles had been. From my jaw down to my legs, everything just relaxed.

"So, in terms of sleeping accommodations," Dad yawned, "you have two options. There's the spare bedroom, and I know this sounds ridiculous, but it's kind of the domain of Lindsey and Stevie, Amber's cats. They've done a little territory-marking in there, if you know what I'm saying."

"I think I do," I said. "They peed in there."

"Correct. Which is why option number two is the living room couch. It really is comfortable. In fact, I probably sleep better on that thing than in my own bed. What the—?"

As the Mercedes left the garage and we waited to pull onto the street, a rapid fire of pulsing white flashes hit us from all directions: in front of the hood, through my window, everywhere. There were so many sudden, blinding blasts that everything in sight became splotchy blurs. My dad was trying to inch his way forward with his hand out in front of his face, like his palm was a force field that could block all that intense light. *Who's taking our pictures? And why?*

Dad punched the horn over and over and the blinding blob slowly parted. We got about halfway down the block and were just starting to put some space between us when we hit a red light. While we were sitting there, the white blasts quickly grew bigger and the cameras again closed in on us. All we could do was sit there and wait for the light to change.

Luckily, it did right then. "Green light! Go!" I shouted. Dad punched it and the tires screeched. The spots in my eyes were finally starting to dissolve as I looked back at the situation we were quickly speeding away from.

"Whoa! Check it out!" I said.

At least twenty photographers stood in the middle of the street, all still shooting their flashes at us.

"Why do they care so much about us?" I asked.

Dad didn't say a thing, which allowed me to come up with my own answer.

They don't.

17

Amber's voice woke me up. "Mitch! What's wrong with this coffee grinder?"

It was still dark, and for a second, I'd forgotten where I was. Even so, all I had to do was take a whiff of the blanket that was covering me to remember. My grandma had knitted it, and back when our family was still together, it was my go-to. Somehow my dad had ended up with it and he now kept it draped over the back of his couch. A light was on in the kitchen that glowed down on Amber's frizzy hair.

"Mitch, coffee grinders are supposed to grind coffee. That's why they're called grinders."

"That's brilliant, Amber," came Dad's voice from down the hall.

I mentioned before that me and my dad didn't hang out much after he left. We actually only did once. Shortly after he'd moved out, he came over on a rainy Saturday to babysit me while my mom went shopping. We built a model of the Space Needle, which ended up being crooked, and he didn't come back after that. The only other time I saw him was when Mom and me ran into him and Amber at the grocery store. We'd rolled our cart past them in the produce section. "Oh, hi," my dad had cheerfully said. Standing there in an orange tracksuit, he shifted his weight back and forth between his Croc-covered feet. "Uh, so," he said, "Katie and Theo, this is Amber."

"Hello, Amber," said Mom, shaking Amber's hand.

The silence was ridiculously awkward. I wanted to just evaporate. I could tell everyone was trying to think of something to say, but nobody could. Finally, Amber, with her hair scrunched into a bun similar to my dad's, looked at me and said, "Theo, I've heard a lot about you." Her fingernails dug deep into the avocado she was holding, making its slimy insides ooze out. "How's school going?"

It seems like that's always the question adults ask kids when they don't know what else to talk about. What was I supposed to say? Oh, school's great, Amber, but I still don't quite have long division figured out yet. Instead, "Good" was all that came out.

Mom began backing away with our shopping cart. "Okay, well, we should get going. Take care, Mitch. It's been a pleasure, Amber. I sincerely hope you two find whatever produce it is you're looking for."

Now, waking up there on my dad's couch after all that time barely seeing him, it felt like my nightmare was just continuing. I focused through the kitchen glare on Amber and peeled off my grandma's blanket. The cracked, fake leather groaned when I stretched out my body.

"Morning, Theo!" Her voice sounded cheerful, but I couldn't tell if it was real or the nervous cheerful it was that day at the grocery store.

"Morning," I said, yawning.

"How'd you sleep?"

"Okay."

"Your dad went out and got a dozen donuts from Top Pot," she said. "Help yourself."

My dad had always been a big donut guy. When he lived with us, there was usually a pink donut box on the kitchen counter, and some of my earliest memories were of him feeding me pieces of maple bars. They'd always been his favorite.

A blond claw of hair stuck out one side of Amber's head, like her hair wasn't completely dry when she went to bed or something. She set the coffee grinder on the counter and looked at her phone. "Well, what do you know? Someone's a celebrity."

"Who?" I said, picking something crusty out of my eye.

"What do you mean, who?" She stuck her phone out at me. "You, silly. You're on the homepage of *USA Today*. It says 'Boy, 11, heroic in May Day Tsunami rescue. Mother in critical condition—'"

"Amber!" My dad's voice yelled from down the hall. "That's enough!"

"Oh, sorry. My bad." She stared at her phone and disappeared out of the kitchen and down the hallway.

I grabbed my phone off the floor and went to usatoday.com. Below a photo of the mini-Golden Gate was the article:

Amid the chaos and danger of the May Day Tsunami, Theo Cloverdale kept his wits—

I heard angry whispering coming from Dad's room. I tiptoed a few steps into the hallway to hear what they were talking about.

"How long is he going to be here?" Amber's voice drifted through the closed bedroom door.

"I don't know, Amber," said my dad. "His mother is in a coma. You are aware of that, right? He can stay as long as he needs to."

Her voice grew quieter but more intense. "Do you know who left notes on the front porch, Mitch? *US Magazine* and *The National Enquirer*. And even some of those reporters outside. They want to interview Theo for money!"

Amber's volume ticked up a notch. "Do you understand the potential payday, here, Mitch? We've got to strike while the iron's hot. Don't you agree?"

"No, I don't agree!" my dad hissed. "What's wrong with you? The kid's been traumatized!"

I walked into the kitchen and opened the fridge. *Potential payday?* I asked myself. What did that even mean? Did Amber think she could make money off my tsunami story? It didn't make sense, but it still brought an ache to my head hearing how she didn't want me there.

I got myself some orange juice and checked my texts. There was a number I didn't recognize. I opened it.

Hello, Theo. My name is Hugh Bloomquist. I'm a reporter for The News of the World in London. We're hoping you may be interested in talking to us about your experience. Of course, you'd be paid generously. Talk it over with your family and have them contact me at this number.

Cheers.

-Hugh

As I sat there wondering if the message was for real, the phone buzzed with a call from Julie. "Hi, Julie."

"Good morning! Are you settling in at your dad's house?"

"Not really," I said. "Not yet, anyway."

"Ah, I see. Anyway, I'm calling because your father didn't pick up when Dr. Kumasaka's nurse tried to call him, so the nurse called me. She suggested that you come to the hospital ASAP. Are you at your dad's right now?"

"Yeah." My heart sped. I didn't know whether to be excited or scared to death. "How is she?"

"Unfortunately, they didn't say. Can your dad give you a ride?"

"Dad!" I yelled, "can you take me to the hospital?"

He jogged into the living room wearing a red tracksuit. "Absolutely," he said. His goatee was freshly trimmed, and his hair had stiff, shiny product all through it. After being hit by a whiff of his scent, I let out a little, gaggy choke.

"He says he can take me," I said to Julie. "I'll see you there. Bye."

"What'd you find out?" said my dad.

"Not much. They want me to come to the hospital right away."

"Then let's go—hang on, did you brush your teeth? No one's getting into the Mercedes with dragon breath."

I brushed my teeth for about five seconds, grabbed a sweater out of my bag and slipped it on.

"Hey, what are you doing? You're still not ready." Dad came up and pulled the hood over my head, tightening the strings and tying them until just my nose stuck out. I could barely see. "You never know who might be out there. It's for your own protection."

I felt his arm around my shoulders, leading me toward the front door.

"And no one's taking your picture, without my permission, that is. Just keep your head down and don't say anything. They might yell something that makes you mad, but just ignore them. Stay right behind me. Hold onto my jacket."

As he eased open the door and led me onto the porch, I could hear footsteps. They were getting closer, and so were the sounds of cameras, lots of them.

"Mr. Cloverdale," someone said, "can we talk to your son?"

"No."

A billion clicks and voices surrounded us, and the noise was growing. It felt helpless not being able to see or hear, and before I knew it, my head was dripping sweat inside the stuffy hood.

"Excuse us!" I heard my dad yell.

"Theo, how's your mom doing?" somebody asked.

My dad's jacket slipped from my grasp, and I could make out the sound of a finger thudding against someone's chest. "Listen to me. You keep my son's name out of your mouth. Understand?"

"Okay, okay, just chill." The guy sounded scared and mad. "Careful of the camera, bro."

"Careful? I should bust it over your head—bro! Get off my property now!" Dad took my arm and led me to the car, shutting my door so fast he nearly slammed my leg in it. I untied my hood and watched him walk around to his side, stop and point his finger at someone else. He climbed in and slammed the driver's door. "Bunch of bloodsucking—"

Dad mumbled a few more swear words and stomped on the gas pedal. After almost backing over a couple of photographers, we shot out of the driveway and took off down the street. I could see two more getting into a car. "They're following us!" I said.

"Oh, yeah?" Dad's eyes darted between mirrors. "You want to play, huh?" He laughed and glanced at me. "Son, that sorry piece of junk they're driving is no match for precision German engineering. Please, watch and learn." He punched the gas, stomped on the brakes and broke to the right, then to the left down a narrow street. I have to admit, he was a pretty good driver. We darted through an alley behind some apartments, crossed over into another alley then took a sharp right onto Fauntleroy Way.

I looked back again. "I think you lost them."

"For now, anyway. Bunch of rodents."

We wove our way back onto 35th and merged in behind a line of Army trucks. "Hey," I said, "have you ever heard of *The London News of the World?*"

Dad looked at the mirror again and for a quick second at me. "I think so," he said. "It's one of those British tabloids. Lots of sensational stories. Scandals. Disasters. Some of it they just make up."

I got out my phone and read him the text from Hugh Bloomquist.

"Interesting," he said. "But—yeah, no, that's not going to happen."

I was surprised by his answer. After all the money-making ideas I'd seen him run by my mom over the years, I wasn't expecting him to say no to this one. "Why not?" I said.

"It's a can of worms." Dad punched something into his dashboard screen. "A kid like you shouldn't have to deal with all the crap that comes with that kind of visibility. You think this paparazzi situation is bad now?

Just wait until you're splashed all over the tabloids and social media."

I started playing with the glove box, opening and closing it. "It's a lot of money—"

"How about if I worry about that, all right? You're the child, I'm the adult, remember? And please leave the glove box alone. I just detailed this beauty."

Some adult he was. Why should he be able to control me just because of how old he was? It wasn't fair, and there was nothing I could do about it.

"And besides, as His Holiness, the Dalai Lama once said, 'Be careful in choosing your opportunities'."

I faced away from him and stared out the window, doubting that the Dalai Lama had really said that.

"Also," Dad said, his focus shifting between the rear and side mirrors and back to the road. "I have a feeling something more…interesting, may come our way."

We sped up the ramp of the hospital parking garage. It took forever to find a spot, but once we did, I jumped out and took off. I wasn't exactly feeling in the mood for that poky garage elevator and my even pokier dad. Running up the steps two at a time, I could hear Dad panting behind me. When we reached the lobby and I got a whiff of hospital smell, my heart-beat turned up.

"Wait up!" my dad called, his Crocs slapping the floor.

I was breathing hard, too, and sweating and shivering like I had the flu. I stared down the hospital's long hallway and tried to calm myself, concentrating on happy Mom stories and feeling my mouth cracks break into a half-smile as I remembered something she'd done for me when I was in fourth grade.

This kid, Joey McSorley, who was pretty big, had been hassling me every day after school. He'd wait for me, then block my way and tell me I had to pay him a dollar if I wanted to use the shortcut through the parking lot. I finally told Mom, so one time, without warning me, she showed up in the car after school and pulled in next to me, right when Joey had me cornered.

"Hi guys," Mom said cheerfully. "Hello, Joey, need a ride home?"

"Um, no. Thanks," he said.

"Oh, and Theo," Mom said, "please hurry up and get in. We need to run back home to get your uniform for the black belt ceremony. Can't be late for that, and the karate school is all the way across town!"

"Huh?" I said. "What are you talking ab—oh, I mean—yeah. Yeah, that's right, we need to get going." I climbed in and shut the door, trying not to laugh.

"He has a black belt in karate?" said Joey, standing there in front of Mom's window with a shocked look on his face.

"He certainly does, Joey. Hopefully it's not going to be too much of a hassle to get his hands registered as lethal weapons. Hey, we have to be mindful of the law, though, you know?"

"Uh, yeah," said Joey. "Yeah, right."

"Well, we're off," Mom said. "Can't keep Sensei waiting. B-bye, Joey."

Joey didn't mess with me anymore after that.

My mouth was in a full grin as I walked into Mom's room and peeked around the curtain. At the first glimpse of her, the tears instantly filled my eyes and spilled down my cheeks. I hadn't been expecting this.

She was sitting up in bed, her eyes open wide and smiling the biggest smile I'd ever seen. She had a pretend-sad look on her face, the one I'd seen her do a billion times before.

"What's the deal?" Mom said. Her voice was scratchy.

"You didn't bring burgers!"

18

The clenching knot in my stomach melted away the second I saw her. "Mom!" I leapt toward her, then stopped myself. I wanted to hug her so bad, but it was hard to find a place where there weren't wires and tubes sticking out.

"Careful, honey," she croaked as I nestled my head under her chin. I could feel her tears dripping down on my hair. I was so happy that my sobs felt more like laughs.

I heard a loud sniff and propped myself back up. Susan was standing at the foot of the bed, dabbing at her eyes with a tissue. Nathan stood slouched behind her, his eyelids blinking a million times a minute.

"Knock, knock." The door opened and Dr. Kumasaka came in, wearing a massive grin. "How are you doing, Katie?" She looked around at the monitors, carefully studying the red, blue and green digits.

"Tired."

"I'm sure. Well, you're doing great." The doctor took a seat on the rolling stool, opened her laptop, and looked at me over her cat-eye reading glasses. "The antibiotics brought your mom's fever down, so we removed her ventilator. She's been breathing on her own for a few hours now."

I felt so warm, but in a good way, like I was in a bathtub where the temperature was just right. Never in my life, even when I got an Xbox for my birthday, could I remember feeling like this. Pure joy is what I'd call it.

"But we're still not out of the woods," said the doctor. "Your mom's going to be our guest here at the hospital for a while."

"Ahem." It was my dad clearing his throat. I'd forgotten he was even in the room.

"I'll take good care of Theo, Katie," he said. "I promise."

Susan's face was doing a terrible job hiding the total disgust she had for my dad. The frown wrinkles had returned and her eyes were little slits.

"I'm counting on it, Mitch," Mom said in a voice that was both raspy and icy.

"In fact," said my dad, "I have some business to attend to today—a couple meetings and whatnot. How about if I leave Theo here to catch up with you since he's been cooped up with me for the past however long. Here you go, buddy." My dad handed me a $5 bill. "Hang out with your mom and get yourself some lunch."

This won't even buy a sandwich, I thought, stuffing the money into my pocket. "Thanks."

"No prob. See you in a few."

"Take your time," I said.

The afternoon was nice. Hospital staff came in and out all day to check on my mom and she also took a nap, but the rest of the time we played cards with Nathan and Susan, and watched Cartoon Network on the room's TV. I ordered hospital pizza, which wasn't too bad, and spent my dad's five bucks on candy from the gift shop.

Dr. Kumasaka was checking on my mom when Dad came back around six that night. He was followed by Sergeant Loden. "Look who I ran into in the hallway," said my dad.

I didn't like the look on the sergeant's face. It was like she'd just seen a monster. "I have some news." Her eyes were glistening when she finally looked at me. "It's about Mr. Sharrard."

"Did they find him?" I sniffed. All my muscles tightened as I sat up and raked a sleeve across my itchy eyes. "Is he okay?"

"I'm afraid not," Sergeant Loden said. "He—um— well—"

I could feel the oxygen draining from Mom's room while the sergeant struggled to finish her sentence.

"Mr. Sharrard didn't make it."

19

Susan gasped and put her hand to her mouth. "Oh, no."

"That's impossible," I said, "I just saw him, walking around—you know—getting all the kids to pay attention— helping them get safe. Teachers don't die." My knees felt like they were about to shatter.

"From what I understand," said the sergeant, "he was helping to lift students over an obstruction by the railroad tracks. He was hit by something in the water, which knocked him out. It appears he drowned. He was eventually found further down by the seawall." Sergeant Loden coughed quietly. "I'm so sorry."

Why would she say that? I wondered. *Police aren't supposed to lie. Especially to kids. And what she said were just words. Words can be wrong.*

But these words weren't wrong, and I knew it. I felt about a second away from exploding into a thousand pieces. Mr. Sharrard was gone. His dumb jokes. His tan pants. His carrot sticks that he ate in the afternoon instead of Reese's Peanut Butter Cups because his wife told him he needed to eat healthier. He was gone. And never coming back.

"Come here, baby," Mom whispered. "Come sit with me."

"He's not dead," I said shakily. "He can't be. He can't be—" I lost it. I could feel Mom's chin lightly touching the top of my head. "Shhh. It's okay," she said softly. "We'll get through this."

After a while, I sat up on the bed and wiped my eyes. "Where's everybody else? Where's Caryn—and Kenny—and—and—everybody else?"

Sergeant Loden rubbed her temples. "Not everybody in your class has been accounted for," she said. "And unfortunately, I don't have much more information for you right now, except that Mr. Sharrard was the reason things didn't turn out a lot worse. He helped a lot of people get to higher ground before the last wave hit."

For a while, no one said a word. We all just stayed in place, each of us experiencing our own silent shock and sadness. I felt like a stiff washcloth, wrung out and dried up.

"Okay," Dr. Kumasaka finally said. "Katie needs some rest. In fact, why don't you all go home and try to relax. You've been through a lot." She looked at me. "Your mom is in good hands, Theo."

"Go back to your dad's, honey." Mom reached over and softly ruffled my hair. "I'll see you soon. Ow! Huh, I didn't realize how sore I was."

I hugged her, probably a little too hard because she tensed up a little. "Okay, see you tomorrow, Mom."

"I love you, honey," she whispered.

"I love you, too." I said, gently nestling my head up against hers one last time.

"Mitch," she said, her eyes stabbing into my dad. "Be a good father."

He shook his head and looked at her as if she'd insulted him. "Of course."

I brushed past Dr. Kumasaka and followed my dad and Sergeant Loden into the hallway. The sergeant was walking really close to my dad, with her head tilted toward him. I eased up behind them, just inside listening range.

"—over three hundred people are dead," the sergeant whispered.

"Oh, my g—." Dad must have sensed me standing right behind him because he stopped and turned around. "Oh, um, hey, son," he said. "The sergeant was just telling me about the rescue operation. Pretty impressive."

Yeah, right, I thought. The guy could think up lies faster than the Grinch himself.

The three of us got in the elevator and took it to the main parking level. As the bell dinged and the doors opened, we were met with a familiar scene. *Click flash… click click… flash click.* Bursts of white light. More flashes. And more.

"Theo!" a woman's voice yelled, "how's your mom doing?"

A guy in a long beard with an even longer camera lens shouted out, "Theo, do you think your teacher's a hero? Giving his life for your class the way he did?"

Before I knew it, Sergeant Loden was up the reporter's face, so close that her breath was fogging up the guy's glasses. A big vein in her neck bulged with every second or third word she barked out.

"You need to leave this young man alone! If you ever talk to him again, if you ever put that lens in his face again, I promise to be your personal limo driver to a nice evening in county lockup. Got me?"

"But… but I'm not breaking the law." He backed up a step and fixed his glasses.

She stepped toward him. "Maybe, maybe not. But let me ask you something: What would your mother think about what you're doing right now? Do you think she'd have something to say if you were having your privacy invaded in such an egregious manner after surviving a highly traumatic event?" She shook her finger at him. "Or how about this: what if your mom was in there fighting for her life? Hmm? Now step aside. And no more pictures."

The guy looked embarrassed, but nobody else seemed to pay attention, as the click flash mob stuck to us all the way to the car. My dad shoved another photographer out of the way.

"You'll hear from my editor," said the guy, almost tripping over backwards.

"Looking forward to it," Dad said.

"Mr. Cloverdale!" a different voice yelled. "How are you holding up?"

"Well, you know, I'm doing fine, under the circumstances, anyway."

Oh, I see how it is, I thought. My dad wouldn't allow any questions about me, but he had no problem answering ones about him. He had stopped by the elevators and had a big crowd of reporters surrounding him. His voice sounded dramatic: "I'm just taking things one day at a—"

"Mitch!" shouted the sergeant from the open door of her police cruiser. "We're leaving!"

"Yeah, right, okay," he said, chirping my door open. "There you go, son."

What a weirdo, I thought.

After he started up the car, the sergeant came to the driver's side and signaled him to roll down his window. "Follow me out. And don't talk to those scumbags anymore."

"Gotcha," said my dad.

We tailed Sergeant Loden's car down the ramp and onto the street. More photographers were waiting on the sidewalk. "They must know my car," Dad said. "It's such a beautiful machine, it's probably got its own Instagram account by now." Flashes exploded all around us, but everyone moved to the side when the sergeant squawked the siren and switched on her blues. I exhaled a huge sigh of relief after realizing this escape wouldn't be like the last one.

Turning onto the street, we stuck close to the sergeant's car. It was pretty cool actually; cars pulled to the side for us and we even ran some red lights. The most important thing was that we weren't being followed. When we were back in West Seattle, Sergeant Loden gave a yelp on her siren, waved at us in her rear-view mirror and split away at 35th and Alaska.

"How about that, son? A police escort," he said.

I couldn't hold it in anymore. "Can you not call me 'son'?"

"Why? You are my son."

"Can you just call me Theo?"

"Sure," he said. "Of course."

We were both quiet the rest of the way to his house, where he turned into the driveway, shut off the car and looked at me. "Listen, Theo, I know I've been a really poor excuse for a dad. And—I deeply regret it." His eyes suddenly got teary. "I just want you to know that."

"I don't want to talk about this right now."

"I understand. But I want to make it up to you."

I was exhausted, and definitely not in the mood to hear him saying his crap in the same begging tone of voice he'd used with my mom so many times before. "Can we just go insi..."

"I've been so selfish the past few years. And even though your mom and I aren't together anymore, I want to be part of your life again." A single tear dropped down and dissolved into his goatee. "And, um, I hope someday, you'll want to be part of mine."

"Okay," I said. "Can we go now?"

Dad grabbed a tissue out of the glove box and blew his nose. "Sure."

We made our way up the cracked asphalt walkway to his porch. *This will only be a few days,* I thought, as we went into his house. *A week at the most. Then Mom will be able to come home and I can start not seeing or thinking about him again.*

We split off, Dad to his room and me to the couch. I kicked off my shoes and tried to think positive, telling myself that Mom was alive and awake and doing great. We would be a team again. And soon.

My phone had 63 texts—from *Good Morning America,* from the *New York Post*—another from some TV show called *60 Minutes.* It was pretty overwhelming, so I decided not to read any of them and looked at my photos instead. There were lots from the field trip and a bunch from the bus on the way there. As I swiped to the video, my finger stopped. Should

I watch it? Yes, no—yes, it was definitely time. I pushed *play* before I could think about it again.

The date said May 1. The first video was Mom chasing after Lucy, climbing the tree and getting stuck. You can hear kids laughing, including me a little bit. In the next video, the view was from the Golden Gate sculpture. Everyone's having a great time running around at the bottom of the hill. I had been so hungry for lunch; I definitely remember that.

Suddenly, the wave shoots up and swallows the Edgewater. I'm yelling, shouting to Mom, freaking out more by the second. But I keep filming. I notice other stuff, things I didn't remember seeing the first time. When the wave hits, boats start popping up in the air like toys. People are screaming and running and getting upended by water. Mom's hanging onto the tree, trying to...

"What are you watching there?" Amber's voice startled me. I could smell her perfume as she hovered over me.

"Oh. Oh, my gosh," she said. "Is that what I think it is?"

"What?" I said.

"The tsunami!" she said. "You actually recorded it?"

"Not really." I switched my phone off and rested it on my chest.

"Sure looks like it to me."

Amber's pink nails brushed my arm, making me shiver. "Honey, you could be sitting on a gold mine."

"A gold mine?"

"You could have a bidding war on your hands for that stuff. Some people would pay a lot of money for it—"

"Yeah," I barked, "except it shows my mom getting washed away by a wave. I'm not selling anything." I threw Grandma's blanket over me and waited for her to leave.

"Whoa, okay, sorry. I didn't know. I'll just give you a little space." The thuds of her steps on the carpet faded as she walked away.

I closed my eyes and tried to breathe slowly, but I couldn't relax. None of this was any of Amber's business, and it made me mad. I wanted to stop thinking about her, so I went through the still shots I'd taken on my phone that day. The first one that came up was of Caryn. I'd shot it as she'd gotten on the bus that morning and was walking down the aisle. She looked right at me as she passed. Her smile was one of the most beautiful things in the universe. The two of us had met before we'd even started kindergarten. Just like Nathan, Caryn's family also lived in our apartment complex and I'd seen her a few times at the park across the street. By the time we'd started school we were friends, even trusting each other with secrets. She'd admit to me how she didn't like Barbies and I'd confess to her that sometimes I still missed sucking my thumb. We'd been as close as best friends can be.

But there was one secret I never had the courage to tell her.

20

In the morning, my heart sank a little when I remembered where I was. On top of that, I still couldn't get Caryn out of my head. At that point, she'd been missing for two days, and I wondered how someone could disappear for that long, especially in a place as crowded as Seattle. Somebody must have seen her.

The kitchen light came on and there was my dad, his hair unbunned and flowing over his shoulders. He turned on his espresso machine and looked at me. "Rise 'n' shine," he said, pouring something creamy into a cup with big pink letters that said *Thirty and Flirty*. A white streak of foam stuck to his mustache when he sipped it. He licked it off with his tongue and made me gag a little.

"Hey, listen bud," Dad said, "I need to run a few errands." He slid a frying pan onto the stove. "But before I go, you want some breakfast?"

"Sure." My stomach growled at the thought of some food. "Where's Amber?"

"Trying to get to work. Come on over here and keep me company, eh?

Belly up to the bar, sir."

My neck hurt from all the couch sleeping I'd been doing. I rolled my head around a couple of times and dragged myself over to one of his orange bar stools. "Where does she work?"

"At the Muckleshoot Casino. She's a card dealer."

The onions started sizzling in the oil as he stirred. "But so many roads and bridges are messed up by the earthquake that traffic is, like, frozen." He slid over a plate of eggs mixed with potatoes and ham and cheese. It smelled awesome. I dug in.

"Hard to imagine anyone thinking about gambling with all that's been going on," he said, "but hey, hate the game, not the player, right?" He got out a tortilla, scooped some of the left-over scramble into it and rolled it up in some foil. "I'll be back in a couple of hours. Go ahead and look through the DVDs. I think we've still got Shrek from the old collection."

Really? Shrek? I thought. I'd watched that when I was, like, four, but even so, it sounded kind of good. "Okay," I said.

He shut the door behind him. I was alone. It was nice that Amber wasn't there for once, laughing at stuff on her phone and vaping on the back porch.

So, whether I liked it or not (and I didn't), this was my life for those early days after what was being called the "May Day Tsunami". School still hadn't started up and I was stuck at Dad's with nothing to do but sleep on his couch, then sit on his couch and try to stay away from him and his annoying girlfriend.

After a couple of days, only a few photographers were still out on the sidewalk, and they didn't seem to be as aggressive anymore. Usually they just took pictures from a distance and they'd stopped following us. The texts and phone calls asking for interviews started to slow down, too. I guess we weren't the big story anymore, which was fine.

What did continue on full blast was the nightmares. I couldn't sleep without having some horrible scene play out, so I started stressing about going to sleep. When I went to bed, I'd toss and turn, trying not to surrender to another, sweaty, terrifying brain movie, where the actors were usually Mr. Sharrard and the missing members of Room 302. Allowing myself to drift off at night became harder and harder. I never knew what might be coming, but I always knew it would be terrible. It didn't help that life had become really boring because there wasn't much for a kid to do at my dad's place. I tried not to go on my phone or watch too much TV, but sometimes it was hard not to, especially the time I was flipping through the news channels and saw a reporter standing on the Golden Gate sculpture. I turned up the volume.

"You wouldn't know it by looking around here at the Seattle waterfront," he said as the view panned around, showing muddy piles of cars and boats, blocks from the water, trashed and tilted on their sides. "But the damage wasn't as extensive as experts had predicted."

The camera zoomed in on the reporter's intense eyes and perfect silver hair. "The wave did not redefine the shoreline as did three other tremors that have struck Puget Sound over the last three thousand years." More video played, showing huge lines of traffic on the freeways. "But it's still bad, very bad. All through the city, the traffic lights blink red. Utility trucks, some from as far away as California and Montana, have been working round-the-clock to restore power and water to tens of thousands of homes.

"In addition, the Army Corps of Engineers is feverishly attempting to rebuild roads and bridges, many of which were damaged, and reducing the Puget Sound region to islands of disconnected communities." Another video clip played of soldiers on the corners directing traffic.

Just as I turned off the TV, my phone buzzed. It was a text from Susan: *Hi, Theo. We miss you! Call me when you get a chance.*

I called her and she picked right up.

"Theo! How are you?"

"Fine," I said.

"Oh, well, hey, listen," said Susan, "I've got something to tell you that might add a little excitement to your life. Well, actually more than a little. Okay, okay, okay. This is huge!"

"What is it?" I asked.

"I'm just going to come out with it. Are you ready?"

"Yeah."

"You're sure?"

"Susan, tell me."

"Okay— so—you're not going to believe this."

"What?"

"Okay, okay," Susan said. "Here goes—Bridgette wants to interview you."

"Bridgette?" I asked. "Who's Bridgette? Wait. Not *that* Bridgette. You mean—like, Bridgette Taylor, the talk show host?" I was so amped up I was starting to jog in place.

"The one and only," Susan said.

"And she wants to interview me?"

"Yes! Can you believe it? And your mom, too, of course, and Nathan, Lucy, Otto and Sylvia."

"But Mom's in the hospital."

Susan's voice sounded squeaky, like a little kid who could barely sit still at her birthday party. "I know. I know. She's going to do the interview from your mom's room. The hospital has given the okay!"

Butterflies, a whole herd of them, started flapping around inside my belly. "When is it happening?"

"Tomorrow morning. Bridgette will be here tomorrow morning!"

"Do I have to talk on TV?"

"Only as much as you want," Susan said. "Just answer her questions and let her be funny. How about if we pick you up in the morning, say, around eight?"

"Um, okay, sure."

"Great, Honey! Okay, I've got to call my mother. She is not going to believe this! See you tomorrow! Wear something nice, okay, sweetheart? Bye."

"Bye." My heart was pounding against the inside of my chest. I felt like a prisoner, trapped in a box with no one to talk to about the most exciting news ever. I was going to meet Bridgette, one of the biggest stars in the universe, and she was coming here tomorrow! I tried to pass the rest of the day reading a Harry Potter book, but the whole afternoon just dragged on. When Dad finally came home that night, I told him about the whole Bridgette thing right away.

"I'll certainly be accompanying you to that," he said.

"It's okay," I said. "Susan and Nathan are taking me."

"Come on, man." He checked out his reflection in the living room mirror. "I'll save them the trip. How often does a schmuck like me get to meet a major star like Bridgette?"

He did have a point. "Well, just be cool when you're there, okay?" I said. "Sometimes you like to talk a little too much."

"No worries," Dad said. "I'll be a quiet little fly on the wall."

The next morning, I was surprised to see that Dad hadn't come into the room wearing another shiny tracksuit. This time he wore a dark green jacket over a black shirt that was buttoned all the way to the top. He topped it off with dark gray jeans and of course, Crocs. These were black.

I took a quick shower and put on the nicest clothes I could find, which were some clean jeans and a blue sweater I'd gotten for Christmas.

The Mercedes crept its way up 35th Avenue. "Are you excited, buddy?" my dad said. The traffic was a little better than it had been, but it still moved at about half the speed limit. As we were about to pass Safeway, Dad suddenly cranked the wheel to the right and pulled into the grocery store parking lot.

"What are you doing?" I said.

"I almost forgot. We need to bring your mom a get-well present—flowers or something."

"You're getting her flowers? That's awkward."

"Why?" Dad said as he climbed out of the car. "It's not like I'm buying her a dozen red roses. I'll get something that can be from both of us."

"Hmm," I said.

He slammed the door and jogged into the store. As I watched his silver neck chain flap up and down, I wished I knew how to drive. Then I could just ditch him and go by myself, and we wouldn't have to deal with another uncomfortable Mom vs. Dad situation.

A few minutes later, the driver's door opened and my dad handed me some flowers and a bag of donuts. "Hold onto these, will you? Think she'll like them?"

"The flowers or the maple bars?"

"Ha, ha, smart guy. The donuts are for us. Help yourself, but be careful of the upholstery." Dad slapped his forehead as his seatbelt clicked. "Shoot! I forgot to get a card."

"I think you're good," I said. "She's not your wife."

"Ouch," he said. "Look, I'm just trying to be a little thoughtful, son—I mean, Theo. Your mom's been through a lot."

"Yep," was all I said. Because if he thought that bringing Mom flowers was going to make her like him, he was a thousand percent wrong and he should have known that.

Another long, quiet car ride and three maple bars later, we'd gotten to the hospital and made it up to Mom's room. It was crammed with TV equipment and people from Bridgette's crew. One lady was working on Mom's hair, and another was doing her face. A bunch of chairs were set up in a line next to her bed. Mom reached out and squeezed my hand.

"Hi, honey, isn't this exciting!"

"Sure is!" I said. "I still can't believe—"

"Well, hello, wonderful people!" It was a voice I hadn't heard since the day of the tsunami. Instantly, I felt a chill, with my mind snapping back to the tsunami and those hours spent cold and scared.

Sylvia entered first, on a wheelchair pushed by Otto. Her right leg was sticking straight out in front of her, wrapped in a huge white cast. "Careful, dear," said Otto. "You might kick somebody in the tuckus, heh, heh!" He pivoted her around and parked her next to me and Nathan.

"Boys, so wonderful to see you," said Sylvia. "Would you be so kind as to give an old lady a hug?"

I leaned down and sort of side-hugged her while she lightly patted my back. "So good to see you again, Theo. Is Theo short for Theodore?"

"Nope, it's just Theo." I straightened up and looked at Nathan, who'd backed away a couple of steps. No way was he going to hug her.

"How are you, Lucy?" Otto said.

Sitting alone by the window, Lucy smirked and said, "I'd be doing a lot better if Sylvia wanted a hug from me, too. Hmph. Not." She turned to the makeup person. "I don't wear pink or peach, or whatever color that is, okay?"

But even Lucy's bad attitude couldn't kill the excitement in the room. Everybody was cracking jokes while people got microphones clipped on and bright lights were set up everywhere.

Susan yelped a little when Bridgette walked in, smiling her famous smile. "Hey, everybody, I'm Bridgette." She went over to my mom. "You must be Katie. So wonderful to meet you." She took Mom's hand. "If you don't mind my asking, how are you feeling?"

Mom's eyes were huge, her face blushing. "To be honest? This is the best I've ever felt in my life!"

Everybody laughed. Bridgette walked around the room and introduced herself to us all, then sat down in the middle chair. The rest of us took places in chairs set up on either side of her.

"Okay, let's just relax and have fun," said Bridgette. "Try not to look at the camera and we'll just be friends sitting around talking. Don't worry if you mess up, we'll clean up the tape for tomorrow's show."

I noticed Dad peeking into our room from the hallway just as a guy came up and started patting my face with a round cloth.

"Oh, and one more thing," Bridgette said. "There's probably not enough room here to dance. Of course, unless you'd like to, Katie, then we'll work something out." She smiled at my mom and turned around to face the camera. She cleared her throat. "Ready everyone?"

"And three, two..." a guy in a ponytail pointed at Bridgette.

"Hello, I'm here in Seattle at Harborview Medical Center with some pretty amazing folks. You may be familiar with their story. They were on a class field trip along Elliott Bay when the May Day Tsunami hit."

I could barely sit still, I was so nervous. But when Bridgette started talking, she was really calm and it did seem like a regular conversation. First Otto went over how me and Nathan pulled Lucy out and how I helped him with Sylvia. When it was my mom's turn, Bridgette got up and sat on the edge of her bed.

"Katie, before we hear about your ordeal, I want to show our audience a photograph of the Edgewater Hotel." A picture of the place as it looked before the tsunami appeared on a little monitor on the floor in front of us.

"See that red 'E' on the roof?" Bridgette said. "Yeah, it's five stories up, and that's where they found Katie. She was holding onto the 'E' to keep from getting carried out to Puget Sound." The camera zoomed in on Bridgette's face. "Oh, and by the way, she was holding on with one arm. Bridgette looked at my mom. "I can barely hold my cat with one arm."

Susan laughed so hard, she snorted.

"But let's back up," said Bridgette, turning her attention to Lucy. "Lucy, you and Katie were partners that day. Tell me about how this whole adventure started."

Lucy described climbing the fake tree and how my mom chased after her and got stuck in the tree herself. Then Bridgette asked me what it was like seeing Mom get knocked out of the tree and disappearing. When I told her, I could see tears in Bridgette's eyes.

"Oh, my goodness." Bridgette sniffed quietly. She looked at Mom. "I can't even imagine. So then, after you fell into the water and disappeared from Theo's view, what happened?"

Mom propped herself up a little. "Well, I was swirling around pretty fast. I kept trying to grab anything big enough to slow me down." Her head turned back and forth, just like it was doing that day. "A large sheet of metal floated by, and I grabbed it." Mom took a deep breath and blew it out. "But it wasn't helping at all. I was drifting faster, and I was running out of options. I could tell from looking at the shore that I was riding a huge surge back out."

Bridgette folded her arms. "How did you keep your head? How did you not panic?"

"I don't know. All I was thinking about was getting back to Theo—that if I could just grab onto something that wasn't moving, I'd have a chance. The roof of the hotel was my last hope, really. I slammed into a pole, and it slowed me down a lot, but it also dislocated my shoulder."

As I listened to Mom going over the details of that day, it hurt my heart to think about the pain she must have felt.

"Holy moly. What did that feel like?" asked Bridgette.

"It didn't feel like anything, really," Mom said. "That side of my body was just numb by then. I eventually worked my way over to the bottom leg of the 'E'—"

"Sorry to interrupt, Katie," said Bridgette, "but let's go back to that picture of the hotel." It came back up on the little monitor. "Just to show you what Katie was dealing with, the water had completely washed over the fourth story. Can you believe it? Anyway, Katie, keep going. This is incredible."

"There's really not much more to it than that. Like I said, my shoulder was really messed up, so I just had to hang on with my good arm." She bent her elbow like she was still up there. "If the electricity had been on, who knows, maybe I would have gotten zapped."

Bridgette put her hand over her mouth and looked at the main camera. "So, uh, how long were you out there before you were rescued?"

"I must have been hard to spot from the air, because a couple of helicopters flew right over me and just kept going. Sometimes I kind of passed out with my elbow locked around the post."

Bridgette's face looked more serious than I've ever seen it as my mom went on with her story.

"The water had receded completely, so now there I was, clinging to an electric sign 15 feet above the roof of the Edgewater Hotel."

"When they say truth is stranger than fiction, I suppose we should believe them," said Bridgette, "whoever *they* might happen to be."

"You got that right," said Mom. "A helicopter finally did spot me and those brave people were able to lift me out in a rescue basket. To be honest, I don't really know how long I was out there—"

"Eleven hours," said Nathan.

"Come again?" Bridgette sat forward and cranked her neck toward him. "And you, sir, are—Nathan, yes? I love that name by the way. From what I understand, you helped get Lucy out of the water, correct?"

Nathan looked down. "I was on the Golden Gate Bridge."

Bridgette came back around and sat in her middle chair. "Hang on a second. Last I checked we were in Seattle, not San Francisco."

"It's a replica of the Golden Gate Bridge—a sculpture."

"Got it," she said. "And from what I understand, Nathan, your left arm became about a foot longer than your right after you pulled Lucy to safety."

A few laughs filled the room, with Susan's being the loudest, but Nathan's face was dead serious. "It didn't hurt my arm."

"Sounds like a dicey situation," said Bridgette, "with the water getting higher all the time. Well done, sir."

Nathan stared at the floor. I could hear clapping out in the hallway.

"So, Lucy," Bridgette said, turning the other way, "what do you think about all this attention you're getting?"

Lucy looked bored and annoyed. "It's weird," she said. "To be honest, most of it's lame."

"Lame? What do you mean by that?"

Lucy kicked her legs out in front of her. "I don't know. People get in my face all the time. Lots of stupid questions."

"Ooh," Bridgette said. "I hope that doesn't include any of my questions."

"Probably not." Lucy sniffed and looked out the window.

"Well, hey, listen, it's an amazing story, but it must be tough to talk about, so I won't grill you all any further."

I exhaled, so relieved that the questions were over.

"Let's talk about something a little, shall we say, 'funner'?" Bridgette said, looking into the main camera. "As you know, our show loves to give things to people who do cool things?"

Heck yeah, I do, I thought. My face was aching from smiling so much.

"We're hoping that everyone here might be interested," said Bridgette, "when Katie recovers, which I'm sure will be very soon—"

Bridgette looked at each of us, her words getting slower.

"In spending a week —

"At Star World West!"

Susan shrieked.

I gasped.

Lucy frowned. "Do we all have to go together?"

Bridgette looked at Lucy with a concerned face. "I guess that's up to you folks. Is there someone you'd like to have come with you?"

Lucy looked the other way.

"No worries," said Bridgette. "You'll have plenty of time to iron out the details. Hey listen, we need to go to a commercial break. It was so nice meeting everyone. Thanks for letting us invade your room, Katie." Bridgette hugged my mom and looked at the camera. "We'll be right back."

"And— cut!" the ponytail guy barked out.

Bridgette unhooked her wires and handed them to the guy. "Thank you so much, everybody. If there's anything you need," she made eye contact with each of us, "promise me you'll call the show, okay?"

"Thanks, Bridgette," said my mom. "Oh, I can't believe I just said that!"

Bridgette laughed. "Get better fast, okay? Bye everyone."

She disappeared through the door and there was lots more clapping in the hallway. Then laughter. *She must've said something funny.* After a few minutes, all the lights and equipment and people were gone, and there we were, the May Day Tsunami people, sitting around in our makeup and staring at each other like no one could actually believe what had just happened.

"Well, we should probably be skedaddling, don't you think, dear?" Otto took hold of Sylvia's wheelchair handles and started backing her out of the room. Sylvia waved as Otto spun her around and rolled her toward the door. "Take care, everyone!" she said. "So nice to see you all!"

The second they vanished into the hallway, my dad popped into the room, still holding his Safeway flowers. He seemed anxious, constantly clearing his throat. "Wow," he said, "that may well have been the coolest thing I've ever seen! Well, hey, um, while I have everyone here, I thought I'd run something by you all."

Dad went to Mom's bedside table, set down the vase and pulled an envelope out of his jacket. "An opportunity has presented itself that seems—well, it seems pretty doggone exciting."

I'd seen Mom deal with this type of statement from him a few times before. The look on her face showed that she was giving him about a 50/50 chance of either lying or leaving out important facts. "Oh, really, Mitch?" She folded her arms and looked at him, her face totally changed from the crazy happy one she'd had about a minute earlier. It wasn't the first time I'd wondered why they'd ever gotten married in the first place.

"Yes, really," he said. "So get this: a YouTube show based in Japan has contacted me and asked for permission to do an exclusive interview with Theo, Lucy and Nathan. And, um, well, they're willing to pay a boatload of money for it."

Mom rolled her eyes. "Mitch, is this another one of your—"

"Katie, it's not. I know I've gotten involved in some pretty crazy stuff in the past, but seriously, this is legit. I even had a lawyer look at it." He pulled out a sheet of paper, unfolded it and held it out. "See? It's a real contract."

I didn't know what to say, and apparently neither did anyone else. Susan's eyebrows shot up, her hands resting on her hips. "How much money are we talking about?" she asked.

Dad smiled like a little kid with a big bag of Oreos. "Okay, wait for it—five hundred thousand dollars."

Mom's hand shot up over her mouth, making a couple of plastic tubes clack against each other.

"That's a five with five zeros after it," said my dad.

"Half a million dollars," said Nathan.

"Exactly," Dad said, "and it's one hundred percent guaranteed. They want to interview the kids for some popular show with millions of followers. As you can imagine, the subject of tsunamis carries quite a bit of weight, you know, with Japan having a history of them and all."

"Go on, Mitch," said Mom, her tone still pretty doubtful.

"Well, here's the thing," he said. "The problem is, it's almost impossible for their crew to get to Seattle. Right now, with all the damage to the runways at SeaTac Airport, only essential flights are allowed to arrive and depart."

He tapped his fingers on his goatee. "But get this—if we can just get to Portland where there's been no damage at all, they'll put us up in a deluxe hotel, all expenses paid. We'll do the interview live and in person, they'll hand us a huge sum of money and we'll cruise back home the very next day. Done and done."

"I've never been to Portland," I said.

"Wait. Back up," said Mom in her crackly voice. "Who exactly is 'we', Mitch?"

"The kids and me."

"Sweet!" I blurted out, surprised to hear myself being so enthusiastic until I realized how bored I'd been lately.

"Whoa, whoa, whoa," Mom said. "Just slow your roll, Mitch. No one's going anywhere until we get some more information. Let me see that."

She unfolded the contract, her eyes scanning quickly from page to page. "Hmm, I just—I just don't know about this."

"Do we get to eat at a fancy restaurant in Portland?" Lucy asked.

"Anywhere we want," said my Dad, focusing his excited face on Susan. "What do you say, Susan? Is it amazing or is it amazing?"

She blew out a big breath and looked out the window toward the Seattle skyline. "It's so much money."

"Sure is," said Dad. "And to show me they were serious, they gave us an advance." He pulled three envelopes from inside his jacket. "One for each family."

Quick as a cat, Lucy grabbed at one.

"Hey, hey, not so fast," said my dad, yanking it back.

"Ow, geez! Paper cut." She shook out her hand. "Jerk," she whispered.

Mom put the contract down, took the envelope from her table and pulled out a crisp stack of bills.

"That's five thousand dollars," he said. "You get to keep it whether we do the interview or not."

There was so much money in the room that I could smell it.

"When is this interview supposed to happen? "Susan asked.

"Tomorrow," my dad said, as if saying it really fast might work better.

"Tomorrow?" Susan stared at the ceiling and rubbed her neck. "I can't miss work. I'm already covering Katie's shifts plus mine—"

"And that's why the timing is perfect," he said, "because I happen to be available to take them. We need to strike while the iron's hot."

Mom straightened up and leaned forward, her eyes closed, her palms pressed together. "Mitch. I'm just not sure I'm comfortable with you—"

"Look, I know you and Susan are feeling a little apprehensive about this. I totally get it." Dad unbuttoned his jacket. "But Katie, please, look at me.”

Mom's eyes slowly met his.

"You have nothing to worry about. I'll be with them the whole time."

He looked at me and winked. "And in terms of the hotel, they're providing us with a suite at one of Portland's finest."

"Wow. Cool!" I said. "Isn't that cool, Nathan?"

He was quiet for a few seconds, then said, loudly, "Portland has twelve bridges that span the Willamette River, while only two road bridges cross the Columbia."

"You see?" my dad said. "My boy Nate is stoked to go!"

Nathan frowned. "It's Nathan."

"Right, right," said Dad. "Sorry, man. Anyway, I'll have them back Sunday afternoon."

Susan folded her arms tighter.

"And you'll both be a lot better off than you were on Friday," Dad went on. "Just think, Susan, maybe you can use it as a down payment for your own place. You always said that was your dream."

Susan's eyebrows lifted just so slightly.

"I don't know, Mitch," said my mom. "You don't exactly have a great track record with money."

"I know, I know." Dad shrugged. "But this is idiot-proof, even for an idiot like me!"

"I can't let Nathan go that far away," said Susan, "well, not without being able to contact him, anyway. His phone was ruined in the tsunami, and I can't exactly afford a new one right now." She looked inside her envelope. "Well, I guess maybe now I can."

"No worries." said my dad. "I've got you covered. I can provide a temporary phone for him. He'll be a call or text away the whole time."

"Hey, wait," said Lucy. "Then I get a burner, too."

"A what?" I asked.

"A burner," said Nathan. "It's a disposable cell phone often used to commit crimes without being traced."

"Yeah, well, not in this case," Dad said. "Lucy, I can provide you with one, too."

He turned back to my mom. "Look, Katie, if there's one thing this whole experience has taught me, it's that family matters most. And when an opportunity arises to do something positive for my family—for once— I'd be a fool not to grab the bull by the horns?

"What bull?" said Nathan.

"It's just a figure of speech, Nate," said Dad. "I mean, Nathan."

Dad came over and put his arm around me. "Theo and I have been having an amazing time getting to know each other again. And son, have I not been doing everything possible to make sure you're safe and taken care of?"

"Sure," I said. I mean, he hadn't been around much, but when he was, I suppose he'd been fairly cool. He was definitely a good cook.

Dad faced Nathan and squeezed his shoulder, which made Nathan stiffen up and step back.

"Buddy," Dad said, "I know you want to go on this adventure with us, right?"

Nathan stared at the floor. "I'd like to see the Broadway Bridge. It was once the world's longest drawbridge and is painted the same shade of red as the Golden Gate."

"I'll take that as a yes," said Dad, giving Nathan a little shove like they were best friends or something. Nathan frowned and looked away.

Lucy rolled her eyes, grabbed a latex glove from the wall dispenser and started blowing it up like a balloon.

"And on another note, Katie," said Dad. "I'm thinking you're bound to have some fairly large hospital bills." He pointed at the cash-stuffed envelope she was still holding. "That could be a nice start, and there's so much more coming if you and Susan agree to this."

The two moms' eyes locked. Their brows wrinkled together as if they'd been practicing. Then, at the same time, their heads each nodded a tiny bit.

"Okay," said my mom, "but I expect you to be with the kids at all times. Is that clear, Mitch?"

"Of course." Dad placed his palms together and bowed toward Mom, then Susan. "Of course, it's clear. And thank you both! I promise you, you will not regret this!"

"And you'll be back Sunday? Early Sunday?" said Mom.

"One hundred percent," he said.

My heart pounded, my palms itchy from the sudden swell of energy I could feel in the room.

"It really is an amazing deal, right?" Dad said. "And it just kind of fell into our laps. We can't blow this."

"Then don't," said Mom.

"When do we leave?" I said.

"Bright and early tomorrow morning. Lucy, we'll just need to get a quick okay from your big sister."

Lucy pulled her face away from the latex glove and sent the deflating balloon flying across the room. "She won't even know I'm gone."

"Okay. Well, excellent then," Dad said. "It's decided! Oh, guess what else? We will absolutely, one hundred percent-definitely have to make a stop at Voodoo Donuts. His head scanned the room. "Anyone ever heard of it?"

We all shook our heads.

"Voodoo is in Portland, and it is legendary. So amazing, in fact, that the waiting line for donuts can be up to an hour or more, any time of the day or night."

"Really, Mitch?" said Mom, sitting forward and adjusting her pillow. "They are just donuts."

"You obviously haven't tasted their bacon maple bar," Dad said. "It's like a sweet and savory morsel of paradise, and it's number one on my very short list of things to do in Portland." He buttoned his jacket. "But hey, we can talk about that later. Katie should get some rest."

"I'll be the judge of that, Mitch," my mom said coldly. "But thanks for your concern."

"Oh, of course, of course," he said. "Anyway, I know I could use a little rest. Big day tomorrow!" He extended his arms as if to herd us out of the room.

"Theo, come here for a second," said my mom. She put out her arms and I gently hugged her. "Call me when you leave and when you get there, okay?"

"Yep."

"I'm still not convinced this is a good idea," she said, "but if you're feeling comfortable about it, I guess I can go along with it." She paused for a second. "Okay, I need to ask you one more time." Taking my chin between her thumb and finger, she looked sternly into my eyes and said, "You're sure you're okay about spending the night in Portland with Lucy, Nathan and your father?"

"Yes, Mom."

Okay, actually I hadn't completely thought about it, but come on, how hard could it be? We'd all just mind our own business and stay off each other's nerves. "I'll be fine, I said. "Remember, I was in a tsunami, too. I just had a different view of it than you."

"Very funny." she said, patting my cheek. "I love you. Be good."

"Love you too," I said, and darted out of the room. Me and Dad took the elevator down to the parking garage.

"Why does that TV show want to pay us so much?" I said, watching the elevator doors open.

"Because—oh crap, here, pull your hood down."

I ignored him and looked across our dimly lit parking level. Reporters were clustered around Dad's car, one even leaning against the back end.

"Hey, jerk!" Dad yelled as he ran toward the guy, his Crocs flapping on the pavement. "Get your butt off my car!"

"Dad, don't," I said.

"Hang tight. I'll be right back."

He walked toward the clump of reporters. Some of them were distracted by my dad throwing the guy off his Mercedes, but a few peeled off and came at me with their cameras and microphones. The flashes were so blinding I couldn't get away from them. Finally, Dad popped through the tangle of bodies and equipment, grabbed me and we both elbowed our way to the car.

"Theo, get in and lie down. I'll handle these goons." He slammed my door shut, but my window was open a crack and I could hear him bellow out, "Everybody! Listen up!"

The noise died down.

"I will answer one question and one question only. Quiet, please. Thank you. Now here's the deal, folks. From now on, if you continue to harass my son or our family, you will not hear another syllable from any of us."

Syllable? I wondered as the sound of his voice bounced off the low ceiling of Parking Level C.

"Or better yet," he said, "I'll sue you for everything you own, including those nice cameras. Got me? Good. Now, as I said, I'll take one question, then we're done." He paused for a second. "Yes, over there. You, in the 49ers cap, it's your lucky day. What have you got?"

The voice was from a young woman. "Mr. Cloverdale, how are you and your son handling the recent tragic news?"

"News?" said Dad.

I sat up and spotted the reporter who was asking the question. Her microphone hovered a few inches from my Dad's face.

"Oh, uh, I take it you haven't heard." Suddenly she sounded slightly embarrassed. A low mumble leaked from the crowd.

"Out with it!" my dad yelled.

The reporter's voice got softer. "Four bodies were recovered after washing up on the shore at Blake Island. This morning they were identified."

My heart plunged to the pit of my stomach. The clicks of cameras and a few scattered footsteps were the only other noises; as the reporter went on.

"Their names—their names are—yes, here it is: Kenneth Gray—"
Kenny.
"Mae Nguyen—Justine Harrison—"
No.
"And—the final body identified today was—"
Don't be her.
"Caryn Maxwell."

21

Everything went numb—my legs, fingers—even my face. It was too much, just too much. Something erupted inside me, gurgling, rising, exploding. It shot up into my throat and I heaved the door open just in time to throw up on the pavement of the parking garage. Tiny specks of vomit bounced off the ground and dusted the inside of the Mercedes' passenger door. A few more spasms shook my body, and soon there was nothing left to get rid of. I sat up and wiped my clammy forehead with my sleeve.

"Oh, dude," Dad said as he examined the situation from the driver's side. "I'm really sorry you're not feeling well, but seriously? What a mess." He pulled a handkerchief out of the glove box and dabbed at the puke around the armrest. "And here we are, the four of us going on a road trip tomorrow. Such unfortunate timing."

What a jerk, I thought. Did the guy not care that four kids in my class had just been found dead? And one of them was Caryn? He had no idea who she was and he obviously didn't care. But I did. And in that dizzy, sick, horrible moment, as dramatic as it sounds, I realized I'd never get the opportunity to tell Caryn that she was the love of my life.

We went back to my dad's house and I watched movie after movie, including Shrek, for the rest of the day. Anything to take my mind off Caryn was fine by me, even if it was just a little. Later, it was another night of half-sleeping. I tossed and turned and tried to think about nothing. I tried concentrating on positive things, like being on *Bridgette* or going on a fun trip in the morning, but nothing was working. I wished so hard that brains could work like computers and just blink into sleep mode whenever I wanted.

Finally, the gray morning light began leaking through the cracks in the blinds. I rolled onto my back, feeling exhausted. My phone said 6:33. The front door opened, and Dad walked in, fully dressed and greased for the day.

"Up and at 'em, son. Big day ahead!" This tracksuit was maroon, the sleeves scrunched back to show his big, silver watch on one arm and tattoos covering the other.

I ground my knuckles into my itchy eyes. The last thing I felt like doing was being stuck in a car with him and Lucy for the next however-many hours. "I changed my mind," I said. "I don't want to go."

"But you have to," said Dad, lifting his bag off the counter. "We have a deal, remember? Plus, I have a special surprise waiting. I guarantee it'll cheer you up."

Deal or not, I knew I had no choice, so I got up, sloppily brushed my teeth, grabbed my backpack and met my dad outside. Parked in the driveway was a car I'd never seen before. It was beautiful.

"Not bad, huh?" Dad said. "A Mercedes Benz GLE 350. It's new, and it's loaded. And guess what else?" He chirped open the hatch. "It's all mine. Or should I say, ours. Check it out."

The eggshell-colored SUV had a soft, brown interior. A center panel was tilted down to make a table between the rear seats, and in the very back were a couple of coolers and a small microwave oven.

"Each seat has heat and massage," Dad said, slipping on his aviator sunglasses. "And I've packed so much food and beverages that you kids will never get through it all. Guaranteed."

"Wait," I said, "so, you just went and bought this car?"

"It's been in the works for a while," said Dad. "I picked it up last night. Go ahead. Hop in."

I sat on the leather passenger seat. It really was comfortable and smelled awesome, not yet stunk up by Dad's cologne.

"The old ride was nice, no question about it," he said, "but it was time for an upgrade. Especially after you decorated the interior with your half-digested maple bars. Just kidding, buddy."

I knew he wasn't.

"But hey, it's all water under the bridge, right? Because this sweet automobile will be our chariot to fame and fortune in the Rose City, Portland, Oregon."

He messed with the dash video screen for about five minutes, and then we were off. Two quick stops later, Nathan, Lucy, my dad and I were crawling down I-5 toward Portland. There was so much food—sandwiches, candy, even mini corn dogs for heating up in the mini microwave. I think I'd eaten one or two of everything before we'd even made it out of Seattle.

"How does the sunroof open?" Lucy asked.

Dad touched the screen and the sunroof rolled smoothly back.

Lucy pulled off her seatbelt, stood on her seat and stuck her head through the roof. "Woohoo!" she screamed as she threw her arms up into the chilly air.

"Lucy, come on back down, please," said Dad. She did, but it took a while.

We'd been on the road for a couple of hours and had barely gotten past Tacoma. Traffic was down to one lane on some parts of I-5, and we were all ready for a bathroom break. We stopped at a McDonald's outside Tacoma Mall, and after everyone had done their business and was back in the car,

Dad closed his door and cranked his head around.

"You guys, I need to talk to you for a second. So, the first thing I want to say is, thanks for coming. I know it's been a little rough lately, but here's the good news: we're going to have so much fun."

"Oh, yeah? Starting when?" said Lucy.

"But in order to have the maximum amount of fun that we can have, we need to take a few—precautions."

"Precautions?" Lucy said, "what does that mean?"

"It means," said Nathan, as he folded a Red Vine in half twice and put it in his mouth, "that we have to do things to be safe."

"We're not safe?" I said.

"No, no, sorry, that's not what I'm saying at all." Dad took off his sunglasses. "Here's the thing: What we're doing is sort of top secret. You know, like what spies might do in a movie. See, this crew from Japan doesn't want anyone following us or knowing what we're doing. They paid a lot of money to have exclusive access to you guys."

I sat up straighter. "I still don't get it."

"Okay," Dad said, "as you know, the paparazzi are experts at finding out where we are. But here's something you may not have been aware of. They can trace your exact location using your phone."

"They can?" said Lucy. "Mine's just a cruddy old flip phone. It barely stays charged—"

"It doesn't matter," Dad said, kind of aggressively. He closed his eyes, blew out a breath and smiled. "Sorry. Look, you guys, all they need is your number. It's easy for them to get it and once they do, they can track your position and find you. But check this out." He got out of the car, opened the back hatch and came back with a box. It was gray metal.

"This container might not look like it, but it's very high tech," said Dad. "Any phone placed in there is one hundred percent untraceable. Pretty slick, eh?"

Nathan frowned. "I've never heard of a box that does that."

"I know, right?" Dad said. "So, go on ahead and put your phones in. Here, I'll go first." He placed his iPhone in the box. "See? Easy."

I looked at Nathan and Lucy, shrugged and put my phone in the box. "I don't have a phone," said Nathan.

"I don't know," said Lucy, taking the last airy slurp from a can of Cherry Coke. "This sounds totally sketch."

"Look, Lucy," Dad said. "You'll get it back tonight after the interview. I know it's a pain, but unfortunately, it's part of the contract. He reached for his briefcase. "Here, I can show you where it says—"

"Whatever," said Lucy. She put her phone into the box and gave it to Dad, who quickly shut it and slid it under his seat. "I'll return your phones tonight," he said, "and until then, each of you gets, as Lucy calls it, a 'burner'. You can call or text anywhere you want, any time you want." Dad reached into the metal box and pulled out a stack of temporary phones, which he then handed out. I opened mine and texted Mom. I felt a lot better when she texted right back and said she was tired but good.

As I grabbed a bag of Cool Ranch Doritos, I stared out the window and thought about our situation. Here we were—me, Nathan and Lucy, three average kids from West Seattle—riding to Portland in a catered luxury car, about to be treated like stars, then coming home with a whole big load of money. It sounded like a movie with a great ending.

Even so, the further we got from home, the less sure I felt about how great this movie's ending would be.

22

Our interview for the YouTube show was shot in a warehouse outside of Portland that looked old and dirty on the outside, but inside was an amazing studio with cameras, living room furniture and more food for all of us. We sat in fancy stuffed chairs on a sound stage and got asked questions about every possible detail having to do with the May Day Tsunami. The people were nice, but the whole thing took forever, a little over three hours.

Afterwards, the four of us went to the Aussie Steakhouse, which was excellent. They had tablets you could order from right there at your table. "How about we split a couple orders of Chocolate Thunder Cake," Dad said, "then head to the hotel?" He looked so happy, so pleased sitting there patting his stomach and drinking coffee. "We are indeed livin' large, are we not?"

I was full and sleepy when Dad's car glided to a stop in our hotel's valet parking area. Since I'd barely slept the night before, my brain felt like mush. It had been a strange, busy day, and I just wanted to chill. We went with the hotel guy up the elevator and down a hallway, where he opened the door to our room. "And here we are," he said, fanning his arm from side to side, "the Bridgetown Parlor Suite."

It was sweet, all right. There was a living room, plus two bedrooms with their own private bathrooms. Every window looked out on nighttime Portland. Framed photos of the city's bridges were everywhere, which made the place super interesting to Nathan. He studied the picture above the couch. "The Fremont Bridge has the longest main span of any bridge in Oregon. It's the second-longest tied-arch bridge in the world."

"You are something, Mr. Nathan," said my dad as he walked to the window and looked out on the city. "Something, indeed."

Dad handed the door guy some folded-up cash and the guy left us alone in our suite. "Okay, everyone. Our work is done," Dad said, clasping his palms together. "Congratulations, my friends."

He walked around the room and shook each of our hands. "From here on out, it's smooth sailing. We'll hang out tonight, hop in the car tomorrow morning and head back north. Sound good?"

"Where's my phone?" Lucy said. "You told us we'd get them back tonight."

"Oh, yeah, right. Absolutely." Dad patted his pockets then stroked his goatee for a few seconds. "The box is still down in the car. Tell you what, I need to run a couple of errands while we're here. Help yourselves to a pay movie or order room service. When I get back, I'll bring your phones up with me."

We all looked at each other. "Why do we have to wait until then?" said Lucy. "Wait a second—did you just say room service?"

Dad smiled. "Order anything you want. Just hold down the fort and I'll be back in a flash, okay?"

"Okay," I nodded.

"Great," Dad said. "I shouldn't be gone more than an hour or so. Oh, and why don't I just collect your temp phones from you. You won't be needing them anymore. You can use the room phone if you want to make a call."

We handed our burners to him, which he put in the messenger bag he'd been carrying around all day.

"How do you use one of these?" Lucy picked up the hotel phone's receiver and listened, a puzzled look on her face. "Bizarre."

"Just read the instructions on the phone," Dad said. "That sound you hear is called a dial tone. It means it's time to key in the numbers. Okay, see you in a bit!" He tucked the room key into his coat pocket and whistled as the door shut behind him.

Whatever, I thought. *He's not supposed to leave us, but it also won't be terrible to get a little break from him.* I grabbed the room service menu from a stack of hotel info, dove backwards onto the couch and switched on the TV. An ad was playing about a ladder that was so much more than a ladder. "Nathan!" I yelled. "You want something from room service?" He hadn't said a word for a while, so I figured he must be still looking at bridge pictures.

"Yes. No. Do you?" he said.

I scanned the desserts. Milkshake, cheesecake, hot fudge sundae— "I'm going to get a hot fudge sundae. Lucy, you want a hot fudge sundae?" I could hear her bouncing on the bed in the next room, then she came back in wearing a hotel bathrobe over her clothes.

"Is that really a question?" she said.

"Just don't get us kicked out, all right?" I said, picking up the phone and ordering three hot fudge sundaes, French fries and Dr. Peppers.

When I hung up, I noticed that the TV was tuned to the local Portland news. "Tonight," the host said, "we're going to show you some viral footage of the Seattle May Day Tsunami, courtesy of a just-released YouTube broadcast."

I turned up the volume.

"This disturbing video was taken near ground zero at Seattle's Olympic Sculpture Park, just as the first tidal wave hit on that fateful day. Please be warned, some images may be disturbing for younger viewers."

I watched as the wave shot up over the Old Spaghetti Factory. *That's weird,* I thought. It was the same view I'd had of things, from up the hill on the fake Golden Gate. And those were the same people—kids—running around. And there was Kenny! I'd know that red hairdo of his anywhere. But even then, it wasn't until my own mom showed up in the tree, trying to hold on, then falling out and getting washed away, that I figured it out.

"That's your video," Nathan said.

It couldn't be, though. I'd kept my phone with me at all times. Some-one would have to steal it while I was away from it or sleeping—

It was him.

"That lying...aaaagghh!" I screamed, ripping cushions from the couch and throwing them at the TV. I knocked the phone off the table and tried to kick it but missed. Even in the middle of my raging, part of me refused to believe it. This man, this dude who called himself my dad, this guy who'd been so sincere about being part of my life— had stolen my video and sold it behind my back.

I collapsed back onto the couch and stared at the old light dangling from the ceiling, blurry through my tears. "I trusted him. I'm so stupid!"

"You're right, you are stupid," said Lucy, "but that was cold."

The video continued in high volume and high def—the screaming, the panic—waves of foamy brown water swallowing people, arms and legs and debris flying all over the place.

"I should have known!" I growled as I pounded the couch pillow. "I should have known! When he gets back, I'm going to—"

A loud knock at the door and a voice on the other side of it broke my tantrum. "Room service."

"I'll get it." Lucy ran to the door and let the guy in while I took some deep breaths. The waiter came in, not seeming to care about the mess I'd just made from chucking anything that wasn't nailed down. He unfolded the stand he'd grabbed from behind the door and placed the tray on it. "Enjoy," he said, lifting the lid off the French fries. "Oh, one more thing."

He placed a folded sheet of paper down next to my plate. "If you wouldn't mind passing this note along to Mr. Cloverdale. Please tell him our concierge found him a room for tomorrow night. The details are all listed here." He nodded and left us to our food.

Instantly, Nathan was two massive bites into his sundae. His mouth was ringed in sticky fudge.

"Why would my dad get a room for another night?" I said. "We're supposed to go home tomorrow." I picked up the note and read it out loud:

Booked: Room for one,

Single queen bed

Inn at Ponte Vecchio.

"Where the heck is that?" I said.

"The Ponte Vecchio Bridge spans the Arno River at its narrowest point," Nathan said. His voice gurgled from the melted ice cream running down his throat.

"What's that have to do with anything?" I asked.

"The note says he's staying at the Inn at Ponte Vecchio."

"So?"

"The Ponte Vecchio is one of the oldest and most famous bridges in the world."

I was in no mood to hear Nathan's trivia, but he was the only one that seemed to have any idea about what was going on. "What part of Portland is it in?" I asked.

"It's not in Portland," Nathan said. "It's in Florence."

I was getting more confused by the second. "Okay, so like Florence, Oregon?"

He took another monster bite of ice cream.

"Florence, Italy."

23

Lucy slammed down her empty ice cream bowl and stared at Nathan. "He's going to Italy? You're serious? He bailed on us?"

"He wouldn't do that," I said.

"Of course, he would," Lucy said. "Hello, he just did." Her knuckle shot toward my chest and I tripped backwards onto the couch. "And he's got my phone. And my money!"

"He's just out doing some stuff," I said.

"Are you really that stupid?" Lucy shouted. "He ripped us off and bounced." She kicked my shoe. "Oh, I get it. Little Pee-o hasn't ever had this happen before. Open your eyes! The guy played us. He's just a scheming loser like every other dad." She grabbed her coat off the floor, put it on and zipped it. "I'm done being a sucker."

"What are you doing?" I said.

Lucy heaved on her backpack and stomped toward the door. "I'm out of here. And this time it's for real."

I sprang up from the couch, slipping on a magazine. "Where are you going?"

Lucy glared, "Where else? The bus station."

"You can't do that. You don't even have any money. I'll call my mom. Or Nathan can call his."

"Hard pass! I'm sick of being played. And I'm tired of sitting around. I've snuck into lots harder places than a stupid bus. I'm not waiting one more second to be rescued. The only one who can rescue me is me!"

She turned and slammed the door behind her.

I could hear her running down the hallway. "We can't let her leave!" I said. Nathan was standing at the window, staring into the night sky.

"Come on! We have to catch up with her!" I said, immediately realizing I was being way too intense for him.

"Stop!" he said, covering his ears. "I want to go home."

"I know," I said in a calmer voice. "I do, too, but you and me, we've always had to stick together, right? We've been through a lot, right?"

"Yes."

"We can't split up now."

Nathan was squatted down, his arms folded. He rocked back and forth a few times, fast at first, then slowing to almost nothing. Finally, he stood up. "Okay."

I wanted to hug him, but I knew that would've set us back even more, so I didn't. We got to the lobby as fast as we could, but by then it was too late. Lucy had gotten a big head start and there was no sign of her.

I ran out the lobby door and looked both ways down the street. Nothing. I jogged back to the main desk. A guy in a green jacket with a name tag that said "Jonathan" stood staring at a computer screen.

"Excuse me," I said.

He ignored me and tapped away at his keyboard.

"Um, Mr. Um, Jonathan, excuse me!"

"May I help you?" His eyes stayed glued to whatever he was looking at.

"Where's the bus station?"

He pointed his arm toward the front door. "Walk down 11th, take a right on Glisan, then a left on 6th."

"Thanks." Nathan was by the elevator, staring at the floor. "Let's go," I said. Since he didn't do anything fast, we had to make our movements matter. I searched for Lucy's body shape, of a thin, tall girl in a black jacket with fake fur around the hood. No luck. It was nighttime and the streets weren't lit well at all.

A few minutes later we were in the bus station. People were on wooden benches and standing around with their suitcases and gym bags. "How does Lucy expect to sneak onto a bus?" I said.

"She'd have to hide in the luggage compartment," said Nathan.

"If anyone could do it, she probably could," I said. We entered the crowded waiting room and looked around.

"There she is!" I said. "Over there, by the bathrooms." It was definitely her, sitting on a bench, digging through her backpack. As we got closer, I realized that a man sitting next to her was talking to her out of the corner of his mouth. He was an old guy, at least thirty.

"Stranger danger," Nathan blurted out.

I stopped a few feet away from her, but she was acting like we weren't there, not even turning her head.

"Lucy! I know you see me. We need to get back to the hotel."

Her eyes finally drifted toward me. "I'm not going anywhere with you, ever, ever, ever again." She tilted her head towards the man next to her. "This guy's going to Seattle. He said he'll give me a ride."

The dude had a huge stomach and dirty, saggy jeans covering his skinny legs. I couldn't stop myself from staring at a red stain on his jacket. "Are you crazy?" I said. "You can't go with him! You don't even know him!"

The guy stood up, his jacket stain an inch from my face. His tobacco breath blew downward, mixing with the sour odor of the packed bus station. "I think the lady's made up her mind." He poked my chest with his finger. "And if I was you, I'd best be gettin' out of here before I personally throw y'all out." His voice got quieter as he looked at me and Nathan. "On the other hand, I've got plenty of room in my truck. I can give all y'all a ride north." He sat down again, this time closer to Lucy.

"Get away from me, creep!" She sprung up and bolted toward the front door.

I gently hooked my arm around Nathan's elbow. "We can't lose her again." The two of us weaved our way out of the packed bus station and got to the street just in time to spot her. I could barely make her out, running away in the opposite direction from where we came. I pulled on Nathan a little. That wasn't smart because now he wouldn't move.

"She's getting away," I said.

He crouched down. "Can't."

"You can," I said. "We have to keep going. We have to catch up with her! We have to stay together!"

"I said I can't!" he yelled.

"Okay," I said. "Okay."

I tried to get his mind on something else, anything else. "Hey," I said, pointing in Lucy's direction, "yesterday when we were looking at that map of Portland, didn't you say that the Steel Bridge is around here?"

"Yes." He stood up. It was working. "The route we're on goes southwest and crosses the Willamette River at the Steel Bridge."

I acted more interested than I ever had about anything in my life. "It's got to be the coolest bridge in Portland, right? Want to go check it out?"

I didn't try to take his arm this time. As long as he was heading in the right direction, I didn't need to mess with him. The pace was casual and Nathan's mood started to get better. "The Steel Bridge is the only dou-ble-deck bridge in the world with independent lifts."

"Amazing. Can't wait to see it," I said, a drop of cold sweat dripping down my back.

It didn't take long to reach Waterfront Park and the lower walkway of the Steel Bridge. "There she is," Nathan said, pointing to the bridge's upper deck, where Lucy stood in the middle, halfway to the other side.

"I'm going to go talk to her," I said. "Stay right here, okay?"

"Okay."

I jogged up some stairs and came out on the walkway. "Hey," I said, slowly approaching her. I was trying to act chill, like I'd just bumped into her in the school hallway.

She hopped onto the railing and sat facing me. Suddenly, she leaned backward, making the bottom drop out of my stomach. She sat forward, letting her hands go and teetering back and forth with nothing but her athletic balance keeping her from falling into the black water below. My knees wobbled as I watched her. Her arms shot out, making her body lurch backward. She grabbed the rail just in time.

"Lucy! Come down!" I said. "You could fall!"

"Highly doubtful, Pee-o. I could do this in my sleep." Lucy lifted her hands off the railing again, her legs sticking out straight in front of her. "I can take care of myself. Nobody else cares, anyway."

"I care." *Did I really just say that?*

"Yeah, right. I'll tell you what. You and your weirdo BFF can just get out of here. I'm good." Her head turned as she looked at the darkness below her. It was impossible to tell where the sky stopped and the water started.

"I don't want you here!" she screamed. "I don't need y—"

"Lucy," Nathan said. I hadn't noticed that he'd made his way up to where we were. He stood about ten feet away from me and Lucy with his hands digging into his coat pockets.

"Shut up!" she screamed.

"I know why you do it," Nathan said

Swaying back and forth, Lucy again grabbed the rail to steady herself. "Why I do what?"

"Why you run away."

Her legs dangled from the rusty railing, her arms shifting to keep balance in the swirling wind.

"There's too much going on in your head," Nathan said. "It's so crowded you just want to get away from it." His knuckles dug into his ears.

Lucy laughed. "Yeah, Nathan, you've got it so rough. I'll bet every morning, you wake up and your mom fixes you a nice big bowl of Frooty Loops, maybe a glass of Sunny D to go along with it. Try making a big heaping, overflowing bowl of nothing every morning. I'm a master chef."

I reached a hand out to her. "Lucy—"

"Get away from me. Whoa! Ha!" Her arms windmilled and she caught herself again. "Pretty hard to fix breakfast for your kids when you're sitting in a drug rehab like my mom's doing right now. But hey, speaking of my mom," Lucy said, her hair flying around in the wind, "since we're here, hanging out like besties and whatnot, how about if I tell you a little story about her? We know each other well enough by now, right?"

The only sound came from the night wind whistling through the old bridge.

"One night, Mommy was completely out of it, worse than I've ever seen her. I don't know what drugs she was on, but she'd been up for days." Lucy's body stopped rocking and she stared into the distance. "She'd already closed all the blinds 'cause she thought men in black suits were spying on her, that helicopters were about to land on the roof of our building. And, well, hey, lucky for me, she decided to share a little family history one night."

A gust of wind blasted the side of Lucy's head, sweeping her hair over her face. She coughed and spat a glob of spit into the dark. "Remember that day at show-and-tell when I said I never knew my dad?"

I stayed silent, scared to death that the wrong answer might lead to a really bad result. She pinched her eyes shut. "Actually, I lied. I really did know him, for a few months anyway, according to what my mom said. Ha! Whoops! Whoa!" The wind blew her hair away from her face. Her lips were shadows. Her eyes were black.

"Well, anyway, Mama must have been feeling extra chatty on this particular evening, because she told me I was actually there the night my dad died."

My knees weren't keeping my body steady. "You were?"

"I even saw it happen, Mom said. I was a baby. We lived in a big house with a whole bunch of people. Everybody partied all the time—well, everybody except the little kids." Lucy swiped her sleeve across her nose and looked at the darkness behind her. Her head turned slowly back around and her eyes locked in on me.

"My father died on the floor, right next to cute little Baby Lucy, sitting there in a car seat, all wrapped up in my pink blanket. You can't say we weren't a close family until the very end, right? Haha!"

"Lucy—"

"And the thing is, why should I hate my dad so much, you know?" She let out a weird croaky laugh. "When I don't remember a single thing about him."

"Please come down."

"Shut up, Theo!" She screamed so loud I swear I could feel the steel under my feet vibrating. "At least you know your dad."

"Knew," said Nathan.

Lucy sat still, tilted her head and glared at him. "What did you just say?"

Nathan pulled his chin out of his jacket and said into the chilly wind, "Theo knew his dad. But he's gone now."

His words slammed into me like a kick to the kidneys. He was right. Whatever father I thought I had was gone now.

Lucy turned her head back to the water below and started slowly rocking, hovering over the water a little further each time.

"Lucy! No!" I took a step toward her. She was going to do it. I lunged for her, expecting to catch her before she could let go. Instead, she lunged at me and we hit heads. A blast of white stars blinded me as I hit the walkway. I heard a thud next to me and opened my eyes. She was on the ground, looking right at me. A gush of relief spread over me, but it didn't last long.

Her face told me she was about to do something aggressive.

Her fingers slowly clenched into a fist. Bringing my hands up in front of me, I tried to prepare myself for—for whatever. Lucy's arm shot up and her hand grabbed my shoulder. As her other elbow slammed against my stomach, it knocked some air out of me, and I felt her bony head drive up under my chin.

Then, for reasons I might never know, I stopped struggling. I was frozen, trapped inside Lucy's awkward, invading grip. She started sniffing, then crying, then sobbing, harder and harder, with her face buried in my sweatshirt. Her arms clutched me like she was still trying not to fall off the bridge.

I gently pried out my arms and we stayed there on that cold, windy bridge—hugging and crying.

It didn't last long, though, because now Lucy was mad again.

24

She sprung to her feet. "We need to find that loser dad of yours, and we need to do it now."

"Find my dad?" I said, rubbing the knot in my forehead. "How?"

Lucy started walking, then stopped and turned to me and Nathan. "Something tells me he hasn't taken off for Italy just yet."

"How do you know that?" I said.

"When I left the hotel, I noticed that his car was still in the parking lot, which means he's on foot. But who knows how long we have. The jerk has our phones and our money and we need to do something now."

"He might still come back," I said. "He's only been gone for a couple of hours."

"Dude, wake up!" said Lucy. "He's not coming back. You understand that he can't be trusted, right? He stole your video and sold it. Oh, and by the way, the fool is leaving for Italy tomorrow."

It wasn't worth arguing about. She was right.

We made our way at a pretty good pace back to the hotel. Nathan had worked up a sweat from all the walking but seemed to be doing okay.

"How you holding up?" I said. "You've been pretty quiet."

"Fine," he said.

In the lobby, Jonathan the front desk clerk was still in the same spot, punching keys on his keyboard. Lucy wasted no time.

"Jonathan, did you see or talk to a guy named Mitch Cloverdale?" She craned her neck to try and see what Jonathan was so into on his computer screen. "He was down here about an hour ago. Man bun, scruffy beard, wears Crocs—"

Tap...tap tap... "I'm afraid that, in order to protect our guests' privacy..." *Tap tap... taptaptap.* "I can't divulge that information." Jonathan was talking to Lucy like he was the king of the hotel and she wasn't worthy of his eye contact.

"Wait a minute, what do you mean, you can't divulge—this guy's dad bailed!" she shouted, jabbing her thumb in my direction, "and we need some information, now!"

I'd never been more grateful to hear Lucy's loud, trouble making voice. Another clerk, a woman in a hotel outfit like the Jonathan's, smiled as she came up beside him. She whispered something into his ear and he disappeared into a room behind the desk. She smiled pleasantly at Lucy. "I spoke with Mr. Cloverdale."

"About what?" Lucy barely let the woman finish.

"Well, he seemed in quite a hurry. He was looking for donuts, believe it or not."

"Voodoo Donuts?" said Lucy. "Was he asking about that?"

"Actually, yes," the lady answered. "He said he didn't have much time, but he couldn't allow himself to leave town before picking up a dozen bacon maple bars. I told him there's always quite a wait, but he seemed very determined."

"Where is it?" Lucy said.

"The closest one is about two blocks west of here, on 15th and Davis."

"Thanks," said Lucy. "Oh, one other thing—can you check the flights to Italy out of Portland Airport?"

The lady started tapping for what seemed like forever. "Let's see," she said, "flights to Italy start from the East Coast. The next one I can find is at 4 AM tomorrow out of JFK Airport. In order for Mr. Cloverdale to make it in time, he'd have to take a connecting flight from PDX at 12:30 AM."

"Okay, then," said Lucy, "he's probably still around. Let's see if we can surprise him. I doubt that he'll be expecting us to be looking for him."

"Shouldn't we call my mom?" I asked.

"What's your mom going to do?" said Lucy, tilting her fake fur-lined hood down over her head. "She's in a hospital bed, hours away from here. Mitchy could be getting away right now. If we find him, we can call the cops *and* your mommies."

"Call the cops?" I said. "On my dad? Isn't that a little extra?"

"Um, hello. I think he might have broken a few laws. He was going to abandon us down here, remember?" Lucy started shifting from foot to foot. "We can talk about it later. Come on!"

Should I have waited and called my mom at that point? Probably. Some adult advice may have helped. The thing was, I was kind of afraid to tell my mom. I had low-key talked her into letting Dad bring us all down here in the first place, so I was really hoping we could take care of the situation without quite so much drama.

I turned to Nathan. "It's up to you. You can come with me and Lucy or you can stay at the hotel and hang out, maybe call your mom."

It was quiet for a few seconds until Lucy blurred out, "What's it gonna be?"

Staring at the floor and scratching his head, Nathan finally muttered, "I'm coming with you."

Lucy instantly took off, with me and Nathan already many steps behind her.

The Saturday night line at Voodoo Donuts stretched around the block.

As we approached, people passed us in the opposite direction holding big pink donut boxes. By the time me and Nathan caught up with Lucy, the commotion had already started. A small crowd had formed around my dad and her.

Me and Nathan elbowed our way through to get a clear view of things. Lucy was shoving my dad all over the sidewalk. He was holding a pink box with both hands, while also trying to dodge her shoves and lunges. He appeared to be growing tired fast, especially after Lucy drove the heel of her hand into his chest.

"Where's my money?" she screamed at him. "Huh?"

"Lucy, can we please go somewhere and talk about this?" My dad's bun was all the way out and sweaty strands of long hair were plastered to his face. He tripped over a crack and flung the donut box backwards into the air when he hit the sidewalk. Bacon maple bars flew everywhere. Some people were actually hit by them. Trying to get back up, Dad absorbed more of Lucy's kicks and punches and slaps while she growled out a string of R-rated words. I finally stepped between them and Lucy backed away.

"Did you think I was stupid?" Lucy shouted. "You punk!"

There was so much rage in her eyes. Even though they were just dark slits, they pierced like lasers. A couple of people helped Dad up, but then held onto him. Five or six more surrounded him and kept him from leaving. Almost instantly, two bicycle police were on the scene and just like that, my dad was in handcuffs.

He couldn't seem to get the hair out of his face, so he just gave up and talked through the messy tangle. "Officer, I really don't understand what's going on here. I was just coming out of the store with some donuts, and this child attacked me."

"That child's name is Lucy!" I screamed. I got right up in his face. "And she didn't attack you! You stole from her! From all of us!"

"What the heck are you talking about?"

I wanted so bad to punch him in the nose, but I didn't. "We know everything you did! We know you stole my video. And that you're trying to escape to Italy, and that you want to keep all the money!" Tears streamed down my face but I didn't care a bit. "You had to strike when the iron was hot, right? I trusted you! We all did!"

One of the bike cops whose name tag said TJ Leal, must have sensed that I was getting ready to do something physical like Lucy had just done. She eased me away with her gloved hand. "Let's talk over there. Officer Schager will tend to your dad."

Lucy, Nathan and I were led by Officer Leal across the street, next to a fire hydrant. "We got a call from the hotel about a possible child endangerment situation," she said. "Right now, our job is to help get you and your friends home safely. I'll escort you back to your hotel. From there, we can make some phone calls."

My dad and Officer Schager disappeared into the crowd of donut buyers and people who'd stopped to watch him get beat up by Lucy, then arrested. I felt humiliated, since he *was* my dad, but also happy because he'd done some terrible things and honestly, my life was just fine before he busted back into it without an invitation.

Officer Leal walked us back to the hotel and I called my mom from the front desk. She didn't pick up, so I figured she was probably sleeping since it was after 11:00. I called Susan.

"Hello?" I could hear the stress in her voice.

"Susan, it's Theo."

"Theo, oh, thank goodness! I've been trying to reach Nathan for hours. Is everything okay?"

"Um, not really." I nervously scratched my cheek. Susan was about to be very mad. "My dad. Well, my dad… he's…um, he's been arrested."

Things were silent for a second. "Arrested? Why?"

"He was going to leave us here," I said, "and go to Italy."

"Hang on," said Susan. "Slow down. This is crazy." The line went quiet again, and I could hear her taking some deep breaths.

"So your dad is going to Italy?" Susan sounded almost too calm.

"Well, not anymore."

"Okay, well why *was* he going to Italy?"

"So he could take all our money and disappear. He was leaving for Florence tomorrow morning—Susan?" I said. "Hello?" It made sense that she'd be mad at me. He *was* my dad, after all.

"Honey, this is not your fault. I should have known," she said. "I never, ever should have trusted that miserable— okay, that's not important right now. I'm coming down there to get you. Did you call your mom?"

"I tried but she didn't answer."

"I guess it is late," Susan said. "How's Nathan doing?"

"Okay," I said. "He's doing okay."

"Just stay put and I'll be there as soon as I can. Traffic should be pretty good this time of night, so I can probably be down there in a couple of hours. Can you please put Nathan on the phone, honey?"

I handed it to him and listened as Nathan gave her nothing but one-word answers. Then he gave the phone to Officer Leal, who talked with Susan while me, Nathan and Lucy stood there like exhausted zombies.

"Why don't you go up to your room and pack up your bags," the front desk lady said. "You can rest in the lobby in one of our big, comfy chairs while you wait for your ride."

"They're not bags, they're backpacks," Nathan said.

"Sorry, backpacks," said the lady.

Lucy was already packed, but it only took a couple of minutes for Nathan and me to get together our stuff and find a lobby chair. They were so comfortable that I fell asleep pretty much instantly. Next thing I knew, I could feel Susan's hand on my shoulder. I opened my eyes to see her and Nathan's faces hovering above me, flashing me back to the time I'd fainted in their apartment.

"Time to go home, sweetie," she said.

I sat up and stretched as Susan woke Lucy up and led us to her car in front of the hotel. Once we were on the freeway I tried going back to sleep, but it was impossible. I wondered what my dad was doing. *Is he being questioned by the police? Probably. Is he in a jail cell somewhere back in Portland? Probably. Was I going to be like him? Probably not.*

Traffic on I-5 was good until we got to the Tacoma Dome at around three in the morning. Stop-and-go traffic at random times and places had become just another unfortunate consequence of the May Day Tsunami. It felt great to know we were almost home and that I'd be seeing Mom soon. Susan had texted her before we left Portland and hadn't heard back. Even so, since it was the middle of the night and Mom needed to sleep, Susan decided not to call Mom's room again.

I was so tired, I just wanted to crawl under the covers and stay there forever. Traffic was pretty good, so after another thirty minutes we were in West Seattle, pulling up to Lucy's apartment.

"I can walk Lucy to the door," I said.

"Okay," Susan yawned.

We climbed the stairs and stopped at Lucy's door.

"Hey." She put the key in the lock, then turned back to me. "Thanks for helping me out. Your dad's a chump, but you're a stand-up dude."

"Uh, you're welcome. I mean, thanks. I mean—"

"I guess I'll see you back at school, huh?"

"Yeah, I guess so."

"See you around, Pee-O," She hugged me and smiled a sleepy smile as the door closed in front of her.

I was smiling when I got back to the car.

"Safe and sound?" Susan said.

"Yep," I said.

About three blocks from Susan and Nathan's house, her phone lit up with a text. "Nathan, honey, take a look and see who could be texting me at this hour."

He pulled the phone off the dash, his face glowing inside the dark car.

"It's from Julie, the social worker."

"What did she say?"

"She said Katie's fever has come back. The infection has spread."

"Oh, no," Susan said.

"And to 'please come to the hospital as soon as possible'."

My heart caved in. *Not again.*

"The ventilator has been re-inserted and she has again been placed in a medically-induced coma."

25

Mom was lying there just like before, hooked up to that ugly thing that made her breathing look and sound like a robot. Dr. Kumasaka was standing at the end of the bed when we came in.

"What happened?" said Susan. "I thought she was getting better."

"She was," said the doctor. "But like we talked about before, bacterial infections can be tricky. We'll need to keep her asleep until her fever goes back down." She looked at me. "Hey, buddy, try to stay positive. Your mom's a tough one. She'll bounce back."

"How can you say that?" I said. At this point my filter had stopped existing. "Look at her temperature—102.1! It didn't get that high last time!"

Dr. Kumasaka's voice was calm. "Your mom is a survivor, Theo. She's going to make it."

I wasn't leaving. Not this time. "I'm staying here tonight," I said. They would've had to drag me out of there.

"Of course," said Dr. Kumasaka. "We can set up a cot in here for you. In fact, we'll leave you alone with her for a little while. Come on, Nathan and Susan. Hot chocolate for the three of us, my treat." The doctor held the door for them as they disappeared into the hallway. "Take all the time you want, Theo," she said, closing the door behind her.

Mom looked so small and helpless in the big hospital bed, surrounded by machines. Until the tsunami, she'd been able to solve any problem, she could get us out of any mess. But this...

"Mom," I whispered, my voice quivering, "you're gonna be okay, right?" Tears fell in thick drops onto her blanket as I took her hand. "We've been through too much for you to die right? Please, don't leave, please, just stay—I— I just— I just need you too much right now—"

I wasn't able to speak anymore, so I simply sobbed, my whole body lurching with each wave of sadness. I rested my head on the thin blanket covering her still body. Pulling up a chair, I sat down as close to her as I could. I hugged my knees, shivering hard enough to make my neck muscles start cramping. I lifted my backpack onto my lap, opened it and dug around for my sweater. A yellow envelope with "Theo" written on it was wedged between some clothes.

I opened it. Inside was a stack of cash with a large yellow Post-It note stuck to the top. The note said:

Son,

By now you must think I'm the biggest jerk you've ever known. I don't blame you for being angry with me. I'd be mad, too.

I didn't feel as if I had any choice in doing what I did. I needed some lead time to get out of town, which is why I took your phones.

A man's biggest responsibility is to himself. For better or worse, it's how the world works. I don't expect you to understand now, but someday I hope you'll understand that what I did isn't personal. Take care of yourself.

-Dad

I crumpled up the note and threw it at the wall. Kicking off my shoes, I leaned back and rested my head against the chair. Maybe it's true, I thought. Maybe a man's job is to take care of himself first. But how would my dad even know that?

He wasn't a man.

26

I woke to the voice of Shrek. He was mad at Donkey about something. I sat up in the hospital chair, rubbed my eyes and wondered why the heck Shrek would be on. My brain was still in a fog, and I noticed that Nathan and Susan had come in while I was sleeping. The movie was playing on the TV in the upper corner of Mom's room.

Mom looked the same as she did before I'd fallen asleep, but now the machine's noise was mixing with the sounds of Shrek, which was a strange combination. Another weird thing was that no one was paying any attention to Mom. I lifted myself from the chair and rubbed my sore neck. "What are you guys doing?"

Susan's eyes were glued to the TV. "We're waiting for someone."

The door flew open. It was Dad, and he was carrying a briefcase. "Sorry it took me so long." he said. He sounded out of breath.

"I thought you were in jail," I said.

"Well, I was," he said, "and here's a bit of unsolicited advice for everyone: Jail is definitely not a pleasant place, so don't make the mistake I did.

Anyway, I apologized, so they let me go."

"That's all you had to do?" I asked. "Why are you here?"

He put the briefcase on a chair and opened it. It was fancy inside; a blue light came on when he lifted the lid, revealing neat bundles of cash piled to the top. Ben Franklin stared up from each little stack, the green of the money mixing with the blue of the light to give everything an aqua glow.

Mom lay there, her lungs inflating and deflating, making the covers rise and fall, rise and fall. Susan and Nathan didn't seem to notice anything else in the room; they were so into the movie. They laughed together at something the Gingerbread Boy said.

"I just wanted you to see the money before it goes away forever," Dad said. He closed the briefcase and spun the combination lock. Then he crouched down and put his hand on my shoulder, his face a few inches from mine. "Theo," he said, "you knew I was going to do this, right?"

"Do what?"

He chuckled. "You knew I'd take everything. Come on, son, don't tell me you didn't see that coming from a mile away."

I pushed his hand from my shoulder. "Don't call me son!" I was shaking. I didn't want to cry but I couldn't stop. "I don't care about you! Or your stupid money! Get out of here!"

He stood up and yanked the briefcase off the bed. "Okay, have it your way." Stopping at the door, he turned and shot me the coldest look I'd ever seen. "Someday you'll learn to take what's yours and not worry about what everybody else thinks."

He disappeared without shutting the door behind him.

"Take what's yours?" I screamed. "It's not yours! It's ours! It's everyone's!"

I wanted him to pound his sorry face. "I'll never ever be like you! Never! Ever! You'll see! You'll s—"

"Theo!" Susan was shaking me. "Theo! Theo! Wake up, honey!"

"I am awake!" I sat up in the chair."

"You were dreaming," Susan said.

"No, I wasn't. Nathan knows. He saw everything. Right, Nathan?" I looked around. No Nathan. "And Mom was lying next to me just like she is now—"

"Sounds more like a nightmare," said Mom, taking a sip of water through a straw.

"Mom!" I sprung over to her, hugging her neck. "You're better!"

"Much better, yes," she said, nodding at the temperature read-out. It said 99.3.

Her voice sounded even worse than last time. "Apparently, those super-powered antibiotics they've been giving me finally started kicking in. My fever went down, and they took me off the ventilator again during the night. You were out like a log, so we just let you sleep."

"And we never left," said Susan. "They found a room for Nathan and me to spend the night. When I came in, there was your mama, wide awake, in all her glory, and there you were—yammering in your sleep."

Nathan came in holding two cans of Coke. "I got these in the cafeteria. They were $2.50 each." He handed me one, sat by the window and looked out at the grey morning. "Did you hear about the arrest?" he said.

"Nathan!" said Susan. She looked embarrassed. "We can talk about it later. Katie needs to concentrate on getting better right now."

"Arrest?" said Mom. "Who was arrested?"

Susan cleared her throat. "Um, well, remember how Mitch took the kids to Portland, you know, to do that interview?"

Mom propped herself up a little higher. "Of course."

Susan stared at the ceiling and blew out a big breath. "Apparently he was planning on taking the money from the interview and sale of Theo's video and escaping to Italy."

Mom gasped. "Italy?"

"But the kids did great," said Susan. "Better than great. You would have been so proud of all of them. If you weren't, you know, in a medically induced coma. Twice.”

“Very funny,” Mom said. “Are you saying Mitch was going to abandon them in Portland?”

“He wasn’t going to,” said Nathan. “He did,”

I showed Mom the envelope with the cash and the note that Dad had written. She read it, then dropped it onto the floor like it was too hot to touch. On the machine, her pulse was going up–85–90–95—

“I just, I just can’t imagine, if something would’ve happened to Theo or Nathan or Lucy– or all three–oh, of all the despicable, selfish– I mean, I knew he was capable of–but this?” She covered her face in her hands. “I never should have trusted him. I am so sorry.”

Susan moved in closer to Mom and handed her a tissue while she rubbed her back. “Oh, honey, don’t cry. We all got scammed. The illusion of all that money clouded our judgment.”

“Knock, knock.” Sergeant Loden entered the room in a rush, her cop boots clunking on the floor. “Hi, Katie.” She held out her hand and Mom squeezed it.

“So good to see you again!” said the sergeant. “Oh, hey, it’s the top of the hour. Nathan, do me a favor and turn on Channel 701.”

Nathan pointed the remote and found the channel.

“Why are we watching the news?” I asked.

“Hang tight,” said the sergeant, “should be on right after these ads.”

Finally, the reporter came on. “Our top story this morning–breaking news: Mitchell Snodgrass Cloverdale, father of May Day Tsunami hero Theo Cloverdale, has been charged with felony theft and child endangerment.”

Dad’s driver’s license picture filled up part of the screen. His hair was up as usual, with a couple of days’ beard growth and wearing a light blue tracksuit.

“After arranging a lucrative YouTube interview for his son Theo and two classmates, Cloverdale is alleged to have stolen the proceeds and abandoned the children in Portland last night.”

"Unbelievable," Mom said.

The newscaster went on, "Among Cloverdale's possessions at the time of his arrest were a passport, a sizable amount of cash and an airline ticket for a flight to Italy scheduled to leave early this morning."

They played a video that looked like it'd been taken on someone's phone. It showed Dad in handcuffs, being led through the crowd while people threw what looked like donuts at him. Half a maple bar hit him in the side of the head and stuck for a few seconds before it slid off.

The camera followed him to the police car, where a Portland cop helped him into the backseat. A flood of flashes washed out the whole inside of the police car and Dad squinted through the back window, looking very uncomfortable with his sweaty, long hair covering his face.

"In other news—"

Nathan switched off the TV.

I rubbed at the knot in my neck that had only gotten worse from sleeping in the hospital chair. How was I supposed to feel about the guy? Angry? Glad? Sad? Maybe it was all three. I knew my dad was a criminal and a total scumbag, someone who deserved to be punished for what he did. But he was still my dad. "Is he going to jail?" I asked, still staring at the TV.

"I'd say there's a pretty good chance, but we'll see what happens," Sergeant Loden said. "Our focus is on you."

I looked at Nathan as he stared out the window, his face blank.

'You helped catch him," I said.

He looked at the floor.

"You're the one who figured out early on where he was going." I tried to get his eyes to meet mine, but it was no use. "So, thanks."

"You're welcome," he said.

"Okay," I said, "but here's the thing—I'm not sure we can be friends now."

Mom's face got serious real fast, her eyes squinting at me. Susan didn't look so happy either. I smiled, waiting for Nathan's eyes to meet mine.

"In fact, we can never be friends again...
"Because now, we're brothers."

27

Seattle Public Schools opened back up the following Wednesday. Angelou Elementary didn't have any damage at all, but Concord, which was down in the valley, had a lot. So, about half of their kids were assigned to Arbor Heights Elementary on one end of West Seattle, and the other were assigned to our school. Concord was close to the Duwamish River and had so much flood damage that it was probably ruined for good. Some kids had lost their homes and were living in shelters. It made me realize how much time I'd spent feeling sorry for myself, while so many other people had suffered and lost even more.

Susan dropped me and Nathan off in front of the school. A woman standing outside told us we should go to Room 302 and take our normal seats. When the bell rang, we went inside, where counselors had set up tables in the hallway. They seemed really nice and encouraged us to make an appointment. I figured, why not? It would be awesome to have a few less bad dreams.

Kids I didn't recognize started coming into Room 302. Since some people in my class hadn't made it out of the tsunami, their empty seats stood out painfully until the new kids started filling them up.

A lady I'd never seen before walked in and put her stuff on Mr. Sharrard's desk—well, what used to be anyway. I had to fight back a powerful urge to cry, suddenly remembering that I'd never see him again.

"Hello, friends," she said, "I'm Ms. Steinhorst. She wore jeans and an Angelou Elementary hoodie just like the one my mom had been wearing on the field trip. "Has everybody found a seat? Please choose an area where you're comfortable." She reached down and pulled a fistful of dry-erase markers from a cardboard box.

"As you all know, we are a new group, so think about introducing yourself to someone you haven't met. During difficult times like these, friends are so important, so see if you can make a new one."

A girl came up next to Nathan and took Kenny's desk. She plopped down a dirty Hello Kitty backpack and sat there with her coat still on.

"Hi," I said to her. "I'm Theo."

"Hello," she said.

"What's your name?" I asked.

"Phoebe."

"Hi, Phoebe. So, you went to Concord?" I knew it was a pretty obvious question, but I couldn't think of anything else to say.

"Yes," Phoebe said. "Concord is in the floodplain. The Duwamish River Valley has flooded throughout history due to its topography and climate."

"Ever since the glaciers carved out the valley during the ice age," added Nathan.

They looked at each other, then quickly looked away.

I smiled and watched Mrs. Steinhorst write the lesson on the board. It would probably always make me sad to think about the people we'd lost. And that's okay. I smiled when I looked at Nathan, then at Lucy, both sitting in the same seats they'd been in before this whole thing happened. And that's when I realized something else:

I can also be grateful for the friends I've gained.

Against the Edge

171

Acknowledgments

So many people contributed to this book. It starts with my sister Ann, reader of innumerable iterations over the past ten years and a creative co-conspirator from day one. Thanks also to my wife Terri, whose anecdotes and experiences as a teacher added so many colorful layers to this story, and my daughters Zoe and Lauryn, two everyday contributors I'm so fortunate to call my kids. My dad and brother, Lionel and Tom, whose senses of humor molded my own, are also on the thank-you list, as is my writing group—especially Nikki, Meredith and Brad—who were instrumental in helping to shape this novel, two chapters at a time. I'd also like to express gratitude to all my evergreen friends, and you know who you are, for being the kindest, funniest people I know, some of you starting way back in Sunday school.

Lastly, to the real Mr. Sharrard, a man who enriched my life immeasurably through his love of words, stories (especially Greek mythology!), music and art. I never took the effort to let him know, and it will always be one of my regrets. Rest in peace, Darrel Sharrard.

Against the Edge

174